Hector Berlioz, Charles Gounod, Daniel Bernard

Life and letters of Berlioz

Hector Berlioz, Charles Gounod, Daniel Bernard

Life and letters of Berlioz

ISBN/EAN: 9783337136338

Printed in Europe, USA, Canada, Australia, Japan

Cover: Foto ©Andreas Hilbeck / pixelio.de

More available books at **www.hansebooks.com**

LIFE AND LETTERS OF BERLIOZ.

TRANSLATED FROM THE FRENCH

BY

H. MAINWARING DUNSTAN.

IN TWO VOLUMES.

VOL II.

London:
REMINGTON AND CO.,
New Bond Street, W.

1882.

PRIVATE LETTERS TO M. HUMBERT FERRAND,

WITH A

PREFACE BY CHARLES GOUNOD.

THE LIFE AND LETTERS
OF BERLIOZ.

PREFACE BY CHARLES GOUNOD.

AMONG the human race there are certain beings
endowed with peculiar sensibility, upon whom
nothing acts in the same manner or in the same
degree as upon other people, and for whom the
exception becomes the rule. With them, their
natural peculiarities explain those pertaining to
their lives, which in turn explain the peculiarity
of their destiny. These, too, are the exceptions
which lead the world, and this must inevitably
be the case, because they are the persons who, by
their struggles and sufferings, pay for the enlightenment and onward movement of the human
race. When these leaders of intelligence lie dead
upon the road they have opened up, the flock of
Panurge rushes in, quite proud of bursting
through the open gates; each individual sheep,

with all the dignity of the fly on the coach-
wheel, boasts aloud of the honour of having
brought about the triumph of revolution.

J'ai tant fait que nos gens sont enfin dans la plaine!

Berlioz, like Beethoven, was an illustrious
victim of the mournful privilege of being an
exception, and dearly did he pay for the heavy
responsibility! The exceptions are doomed by
fate to suffer, and to make others suffer also.
How can the crowd (that *profanum vulgus* which
Horace so cordially detested) be expected to
recognise and confess itself incompetent before
the diminutive audacity, purely personal, which
has the hardihood to give the lie direct to inveterate habits and prevailing routine? Did
not Voltaire, man of mind as he was, did not
Voltaire say that nobody was possessed of as
much mind as all the world? And is not
universal suffrage, that grand conquest of our
own time, the unquestionable verdict of the
collective sovereign? Is not the voice of the
people the voice of God?

Meanwhile, history, which is always pro-
gressing, and which from time to time does
justice to a goodly number of counterfeits of the
truth, history teaches us that everywhere, in all
paths of life, light proceeds from the individual

to the multitude, and not from the multitude to
the individual; from the learned individual to
the ignorant mass, and not from the ignorant
mass to the learned individual; from the sun to
the planets, not from the planets to the sun.
Would you have thirty-six million blind people
represent a telescope, or thirty-six million sheep
make a shepherd? How! Was it the crowd, then,
that made Raphael and Michael Angelo, Mozart
and Beethoven, Newton and Galileo? The
crowd! Why, it spends its life in believing
and disbelieving, in condemning its predilections
and its repugnances by turn, and would you have
it a judge ? Would you that this wavering and
contradictory jurisdiction should be an infallible
magistracy? Go to, that is ridiculous. The
crowd scourges and crucifies, *at first*, but is sure
to reverse its own decisions by a tardy repentance, not, as a rule, the repentance of a contemporaneous generation, but of its successor
and successors, and on the tomb of genius are
showered the crowns of immortelles which were
denied to its brow. The final judge, posterity,
is but a superposition of successive minorities;
the majorities are the conservatories of the
status quo ; I bear them no grudge for it; it is
evidently their proper function in the general
mechanism of things; they keep hold of the

chariot, but they do not make it advance; they are the curbs when they are not the ruts. Contemporary success is very often only a question of fashion; it proves that the work is on a level with the epoch, but does not in the least guarantee that it will outlive it. There is, therefore, nothing to be proud of in the achievement of it.

Berlioz was a man all of a piece, without concessions or compromises; he belonged to the "Alcestis" class, and naturally had the "Orontes" order against him. God knows that the race of "Orontes" is a numerous one! He was considered whimsical, snappish, snarlish, and I know not what else. But, by the side of this excessive sensibility pushed to the extreme of irritability, one must take into account the irritating things, the personal ordeals, the thousand rebuffs undergone by his proud soul, so incapable of grovelling complacency and cowardly cringing; he is always the same, and if his judgments appeared harsh to those whom they reached, they would never be attributed to that shameful motive, jealousy, which was so incompatible with the lofty proportions of his noble, generous, and loyal nature.

The ordeals which Berlioz had to undergo as a competitor for the grand prize of Rome were

the faithful image, and, as it were, the prophetic
prelude of those which he had to encounter
throughout the rest of his career. He competed on as many as four occasions, and did not
gain the prize until 1830, when he was twenty-
seven years of age, and then only by dint of
sheer perseverance, and in spite of the obstacles
of all kinds which he had to surmount. In the
same year that he carried off the prize with his
cantata, *Sardanapale*, he brought out a work
which showed the exact measure of his artistic
development, whether considered in the light of
conception, colour, or experience. His *Symphonie
Fantastique* (an episode in the life of an artist)
was a veritable event in music, the importance
of which was testified to alike by the fanatical
admiration of some, and the violent opposition
of others. However open to discussion such a
work might be, it reveals, so far as the youth
who produced it is concerned, faculties of inven-
tion absolutely superior, and the powerful poetic
sentiment which is met with in all his works.
Berlioz introduced into the musical world very
many important effects and orchestral combinations unknown before his time, of which several
illustrious composers have made use; he revo-
lutionized the domain of instrumentation, and
in this subject, at least, he may be said to have

founded a " school." And notwithstanding this
and in spite of some brilliant triumphs, Berlioz
was the subject of opposition, in France and
abroad alike, during the whole of his life; in
the face of performances to which his personal
direction as an eminent conductor, and his in-
defatigable energy imparted so many chances of
success, and so many elements of enlightenment,
he never had any but a partial and limited
following. The " public," that " everybody "
which endows success with the character of
popularity, failed him ; Berlioz died from the
procrastination of popularity. *Les Troyens*, a
work which he foresaw would prove a source of
endless annoyance to him, completed the fatal
work. It may be said of him, as of his heroic
namesake Hector, that he perished beneath the
walls of Troy.

With Berlioz every impression and every
feeling was carried to extremities ; he only knew
joy and sorrow at the pitch of delirium ; as he
said of himself, he was a " volcano." Sensibility
carries us as far in sorrow as in joy ; Tabor and
Golgotha have a bond of union. Happiness
does not consist of the absence of suffering any
more than genius consists of the absence of
defects.

Great geniuses suffer, and are bound to suffer,.

but they are not objects of pity; they have experienced a degree of delirium undreamt of by other men, and if they have wept for sorrow, they have also shed tears of ineffable joy. That alone is a paradise which is never paid for at its true value.

Berlioz was one of the profoundest emotions of my youth. He was fifteen years my senior, and was thirty-four years of age at the time when I, a lad of nineteen, was studying composition at the Conservatoire under Halévy. I still remember the impression then made upon me by Berlioz himself and by his works, rehearsals of which frequently took place in the concert-room of the Conservatoire. Hardly had my master Halévy corrected my lesson, than I was off in hot haste to ensconce myself in a corner of the concert-room, where I intoxicated myself with this weird, passionate, convulsive music, which unfolded to my gaze horizons so new and so vivid in colour. One day, among others, I had been present at a rehearsal of the symphony, *Roméo et Juliette*, then unpublished, but on the eve of being brought out by Berlioz for the first time in public. I was so struck with the breadth of the grand *finale* of the reconciliation of the Montagues and the Capulets, that I carried away with me in my memory the whole of the superb phase put into the mouth of Friar Lawrence, *" Jurez tous par l'auguste symbole! "*

A few days afterwards I called upon Berlioz, and, sitting down to the piano, I played the entire phrase.

He opened his eyes, and, looking at me fixedly, said—

" Where the devil did you get hold of that? "

" At one of your rehearsals," I replied.

He could scarcely believe his ears.

The total number of works composed by Berlioz is considerable. Already, thanks to the initiative of two valiant conductors, MM. Jules Pasdeloup and Edouard Colonne, the public of our day has been enabled to make the acquaintance of many of the vast conceptions of this great artist. The *Symphonie Fantastique*, the *Roméo et Juliette* symphony, *L'Enfance du Christ*, three or four grand overtures, the *Requiem*, and above all, the magnificent *Damnation de Faust*, which, ten years ago, drew forth such veritable transports of enthusiasm that the ashes of Berlioz must have been stirred, if indeed the ashes of the dead can stir. And yet how large a field for exploration still remains open! Are we not to hear the *Te Deum*, for example, so grandiose in conception? And can no Director be found to give a place in his *répertoire* to that

·charming opera, *Béatrice et Bénédict?* The experiment, in the present revulsion of feeling in favour of Berlioz, would have a great chance of success, without possessing the merit and the dangers of audacity; it would be a clever stroke of business to take advantage of it.

The letters now published possess a two-fold attraction; they have none of them been published, and they are all written under the sway of that absolute sincerity which is a perpetual necessity in friendship. A feeling of regret will, undoubtedly, be caused by the presence among them of certain signs of a want of deference towards men whose talent would seem to place them out of reach of irreverent and unjust epithets. It will be considered, and reasonably so, that Berlioz would have done well to have refrained from calling Bellini a "little shrimp," and that the designation of ·"illustrious dotard," applied to Cherubini with evident malice, was ill-suited to the exceptional musician whom Beethoven regarded as the foremost composer of his age, and to whom he, Beethoven, that giant of symphony, paid signal honour by humbly submitting to him the manuscript of the *Messe Soleunelle*, Op. 123, asking him at the same time to favour him with his observations upon it.

However this may be, and in spite of the blots for which a cross-grained temper is alone responsible, these letters possess a most lively interest. In them Berlioz displays himself, so to speak, *in puris naturalibus;* he gives himself up to all his experiences; he enters into the most confidential details of his existence as a man and an artist; in a word, he unfolds his soul to his friend without reserve, and that in terms of effusion, tenderness, and warmth which show how worthy these two friends were of each other, and how completely they were made to understand each other. To understand each other! These words recall the immortal fable of our divine La Fontaine, *Les Deux Amis.*

To understand each other! To enter into that perfect communion of feeling, thought, and solicitude to which is given the sweetest names in human language—Love and Friendship! Therein lies all the charm of life, and it is also the most powerful attraction of this *written life,* the conversation between the absent, so rightly called *correspondence.*

If the works of Berlioz have led to his being admired, the publication of these letters will do better still—they will make him beloved, and that is the best of all things here below.

PREFACE TO THE FRENCH EDITION.

THE life of Berlioz is only known to us through the *Mémoires* which he published during his life-time, not for the mere pleasure of writing a series of confessions, but to leave behind him an exact biographical notice which, by its recital of his struggles and his mortifications, might serve as a course of instruction to youthful composers. Consequently, while entering into the details of his artistic career, he avoided any confidential disclosures about his private life. He omitted the most interesting particulars, and even when he narrated certain episodes, he did it under every possible restriction, or presented them under a dramatic aspect which deprived them of their greatest charm, sincerity of expression. In many respects it would have been difficult for him to have acted otherwise. If it is permissible in an author to hide personal facts under the fiction of romance, there is always something painful in the spectacle of a man of talent abusing his celebrity by unfolding the intimate relations of his life to the public gaze, and scattering before him the contents of his secret drawer. Berlioz, therefore, only recounted what he could set down without injury to his dignity. But posterity is bound by less reserve, especially when such a life as this presents itself, brimful of exceptional agitation and the torments of a genius unfathomed and oppressed.

One part of the Unpublished Correspondence of Berlioz,* collected and recently published with great care by M. Daniel Bernard, threw a certain amount of light upon a number of points left in obscurity in the *Mémoires*. But these letters only tell us of his works and his travels. They do not reveal to us the Berlioz of whom we get a glimpse in the *Mémoires;* the fiery nature, burning for the artistic fray, there expands in bitter reclamation; his heart remains a sealed book, and discloses none of the secrets which agitate it; his mind does not allow us to be witnesses of the unfolding and development of the conceptions which haunt him.

Berlioz really and sincerely opened his soul to

* Volume I. of this edition.

but one person, Humbert Ferrand. Among all
who surrounded him with their solicitude, he
does not seem to have found one more devoted
to him; surely he it was whom he loved best.
From their earliest meeting in 1823, up to his
death in 1869, nothing shook the deep affection
he bore him. Separated, one from the other,
by the busy whirl of a career in course of con-
struction, or by the anxieties consequent on the
interests confided to their care, only finding
opportunities of meeting at rare intervals,
Berlioz and Ferrand were compelled to have
recourse to an active and most detailed correspondence in order to keep themselves mutually
informed of the most trivial incidents of their
lives. For Berlioz especially, very expansive,
prone to enthusiasm, fretting against the difficulties of his position, swayed by an excessively
fertile imagination, this was an absolute necessity. His correspondence with Humbert Ferrand, embracing nearly all his life, consequently
became an autobiography, all the more interesting because it was written from day to day,
apart from all thought of the outside world.

THE PRIVATE CORRESPONDENCE OF HECTOR BERLIOZ.

I.

To M. Humbert Ferrand, at Paris.

CÔTE-SAINT-ANDRÉ, JUNE 10, 1825.*

MY DEAR FERRAND,

I am no sooner away from the capital than I feel an irresistible need of converse with you. I myself proposed that you should not write to me until a fortnight after my departure, so that I might not then have to remain for too long a time without news of you, but I am now

* Berlioz was at this time twenty-two years of age, at that critical epoch in the life of an artist and a writer when, his vocation getting the better of ill-defined aspirations, his future is irrevocably decided. He had just had performed at Saint-Roch a mass for full orchestra which brought him in nothing, but which intensified his resolve to devote himself exclusively to music. As against this, he failed in the competition for the prize of Rome, and his want of success determined his family to discontinue the modest allowance they made him with the object of his studying medicine. Simultaneously with his rejoicing over having asserted his talent, and his pride at having for the first time drawn the attention of the public and the press to his name, commenced those embarrassments which, to his latest day, burdened his life. He repaired in hot haste to Côte-Saint-André, his native town, in order to avert the storm which menaced him after his defeat at the Institut.

going to ask you to write as soon as possible, because I hope that you will not be lazy enough to write merely once to me, and then to let me languish for two months, like the man of sorrow who, far from the rock of Hope, longed to go to Tortoni's for a vanille ice (*Portier in. lib.* Blousac, p. 32).

I have taken a somewhat wearisome trip to *Tarare;* there, having alighted to make the ascent on foot, I found myself, as it were in spite of myself, engaged in conversation with two youths who had a *dilettante* appearance, and, as such, were unapproachable so far as I was concerned. They began by informing me that they were on their way to Mount St. Bernard for the purpose of landscape painting, and that they were pupils of MM. Guérin and Gros. On this, I in my turn told them that I was a pupil of Lesueur; they complimented me highly on the talent and character of my master, and while we were talking, one of the pair took to humming a chorus out of the *Danaïdes.*

"The *Danaïdes!*" I exclaimed. "Then you are not a *dilettante?*"

"A *dilettante*, I?" he replied. "I have seen Dérivis and Madame Branchu thirty-four times in the *rôles* of Danaüs and Hypermnestra."

"Oh—!"

And we were on the best of terms without further preamble.

"Ah! sir, Madame Branchu! Ah! Monsieur Dérivis! What talent! What tragic force!"

"I know Dérivis very well," said the other.

"And I have the advantage of knowing the sublime lyric actress equally well."

"Ah, sir, you are fortunate indeed! I am told that, independently of her marvellous talent, she is most remarkable for her wit and her moral excellency."

"Assuredly; nothing could be more true."

"But, gentlemen," I said to them, "how comes it that you, who are not musicians by profession, have not been infected by the *dilettante* poison, and that Rossini has not made you turn your backs upon what is natural and in accordance with common-sense?"

"Because," they replied, "having become accustomed to seek in painting for what is grand, beautiful, and, above all, natural, we have not been able to disown it in the sublime pictures of Glück and Saliéri, any more than in the accents, at once, tender, heart-rending, and terrible, of Madame Branchu and her worthy rival. Consequently, the style of music now in vogue has no more attraction for us than the arabesques or the sketches of the Flemish school would have."

That is something like, my dear Ferrand, that is something like! Here you have men who can feel, good judges who are fit to go to the Opéra, capable of hearing and understanding *Iphigénie en Tauride.* We exchanged addresses, and shall meet again in Paris on our return.

Have you seen *Orphée* again, with M. Nivière, and have you succeeded in getting hold of it to any extent?

Adieu.   All is going on well with me; my father is completely on my side, and my mother is already talking calmly of my return to Paris.

II.

PARIS, NOVEMBER 29, 1827.

MY DEAR FERRAND,

Your silence with regard to me, as well as to Berlioz * and Gounet, is inexplicable.   I know that you have been ill again; several people have told me so, but was not your brother's pen at hand to let us know of your convalescence?   Why leave us in such anxiety? For some time past we have been under the impression that you had set out for Switzerland.

* Auguste Berlioz.

"But," I have been constantly saying to myself, "even if that should be so, I see no reason
for his not writing. There is a post in Switzerland as elsewhere."

I fancy, therefore, that your silence must be
attributed, not to forgetfulness, but to that care-
lessness mingled with laziness of which you
have so large a share. I hope, nevertheless,
that you will regain sufficient activity to allow
of your replying to me.

My *Mass* was performed on St. Cecilia's day
with twice the success which attended the first
representation; the small corrections I made in
it have improved it materially, the passage

Et iterum venturus

especially, which was ruined on the first occasion, was interpreted this time in a most striking
manner by six trumpets, four French horns,
three trombones, and two ophicleides. The
chorus which follows, and which was sung by
all the voices in unison,

Cuivre.

with a chord for brass instruments half-way
through, produced a tremendous impression
upon everybody. As far as I was concerned, I
had up to this point maintained my self-posses-
sion, and it was of the utmost importance that
I should remain cool. I was leading the orchestra, but, when I saw this picture of the Last
Judgment, the announcement sung by six bass
voices in unison, the awful *clangor tubarum*, the
shouts of fear from the multitude represented
by the chorus, everything in short rendered
precisely as I had conceived it, I was seized with
a convulsive trembling which I had just sufficient strength to subdue up to the end of the
passage, but which then compelled me to sit
down and to allow my orchestra to rest for some
moments; I could no longer stand, and I feared
lest my *báton* should fall from my hand. Ah!
if you had only been there ! I had a magnificent orchestra, and had summoned forty-five
violins; thirty-two came, with eight violas, ten
violoncellos, and eleven double-basses. Unfortunately, I had not enough voices, especially for
an immense church like Saint-Eustache. The
Corsaire and *Pandore* praised me, but without
going into detail about things which, as the
saying goes, are " caviare to the general." I
am awaiting the judgment of Castil-Blaze, who

promised me that he would be present, of Fétis
and the *Observateur;* they are the only newspapers to which I sent invitations, the others
being too much taken up with politics.

I made my appearance at a most unfortunate
moment; many whom I had invited, amongst
others the ladies Lefranc, did not come on account of the frightful disturbances of which the
Quartier Saint-Dénis has been the scene during
the last few days. But, be that as it may, I
succeeded beyond my expectations, and I have
really a following at the Odéon, the Bouffes
the Conservatoire, and the Gymnase. I have
been congratulated on all sides, and on the very
evening of the performance I received a com-
plimentary letter from a gentleman whom I do
not know, but who wrote most charmingly. I
have sent invitations to all the members of the
Institut, and I was delighted that they should
hear the performance of what they call impracticable music, for my *Mass* is thirty times more
difficult than the *cantata* I sent in for the competition, and you know that I was compelled to
withdraw that because M. Rifaut was unable to
play it on the piano, and M. Berton was em-
phatic in declaring that it was incapable of
being performed, even by an orchestra.

My great crime (at all events at present) in the eyes of this old and cold classic is my seeking to produce something new.

"That is a chimera, my dear fellow," he said to me a month ago; "there is nothing new in music; the great masters adhered to certain musical forms which you will not adopt. Why seek to do better than the great masters? And as I know that you entertain a great admiration for a man who, certainly, is not destitute of talent and genius—I mean Spontini"—

"Oh! yes, I have a great admiration for him, and always shall have."

"Well, my dear fellow, Spontini, in the eyes of veritable *connoisseurs*, is not very highly esteemed."

Upon that, as you may well imagine, I lost all respect for him. The old imbecile! If that is my crime, I must confess that it is a serious one, for never was admiration more sincere or with a better foundation; nothing can equal it except, indeed, the contempt I feel for the petty jealousy of the academician.

Must I demean myself so far as to compete once more? I must, for my father wishes it, and attaches much importance to the prize. For his sake I will be represented, and will write them a homely composition which will be quite as effective when played on the piano as by the richest orchestra; I will be lavish in redundancies, *because they are the forms to which the great masters adhered, and one must not do better than the great masters*, and if I gain the prize, I swear to you that I will tear up my *Scène* before the very eyes of these gentlemen as soon as the prize has been awarded to me.

I write warmly to you about all this, my dear friend, but you have no idea how little importance I attach to it. For three months I have been a prey to grief from which nothing can distract me, and my disgust with life is unsurpassable. Even the success I have just gained only momentarily removed the grievous weight which oppresses me, and now it has come back, and the oppression is greater than before. I cannot in this letter supply you with the key to the enigma; it would be too long a tale, and, moreover, I verily believe that I should be unable to trace the characters in which to write to you on such a subject. When we meet again you shall know all. I conclude with the speech which the ghost of the King of Denmark addresses to his son Hamlet :—

Farewell, farewell, remember me !

III.

PARIS, FRIDAY, JUNE 6, 1828.

MY DEAR FRIEND,

You are, no doubt, all impatience to learn the result of my concert; if I have not written to you sooner, it has been simply on account of my preferring to wait for the verdict of the newspapers. All those which have made any mention of me, except the *Revue Musicale* and the *Quotidienne*, which I have not yet been able to procure, should reach you at the same time as this letter.

A great, great success ! A success produced by astonishment in the public mind, and enthusiasm among artists.

I was so warmly applauded at the general rehearsals on Friday and Saturday that I was not at all uneasy about the effect which my music would produce upon the paying portion of the public. The overture to *Waverley*, which you do not know, inaugurated the entertainment in the most favourable manner possible, seeing that it received three rounds of applause. After it came our favourite *Mélodie Pastorale*. It was very badly sung by the soloists, and and chorus at the end was a signal failure. The singers, instead of counting their pauses, waited for a signal which the leader of the orchestra did not give them, and they only perceived that they had not come in at the proper moment when the passage was almost concluded. Altogether, this portion did not produce one quarter the effect it really possesses.

The *Marche religieuse des Mages*, also unknown to you, was loudly applauded. But, when it came to the *Resurrexit* from my mass, which you have not heard since I put the finishing touches to it, and which was sung by fourteen female and thirty male voices, the concert-room of the Royal School of Music witnessed for the first time the spectacle of the members of the orchestra rising from their seats after the last chord, and applauding more vigorously than the public. The taps of the bows sounded like hail upon the violoncellos and double bases; the chorus, male and female, applauded alike; when one round was finished another commenced; voices shouted and feet stamped upon the floor!

At last, no longer able to keep quiet in my corner of the orchestra, I leaned my head on the kettle-drums and cried like a child.

Ah! why were you not there, dear friend? You would have witnessed the triumph of a cause which you have so warmly defended against the narrow-minded and short-sighted. In truth, at the moment when my emotion was at its height, I thought of you, and could not help groaning over your absence.

The second part commenced with the overture to the *Francs Juges*. I must tell you what happened at the first rehearsal of this movement. Scarcely had the orchestra heard that terrible solo for trombone and ophicleide in the third act, for which you wrote the words for Olmerick,

than one of the violins exclaimed—

" Ah ! ah ! The rainbow is the bow of your violin, the winds play the organ, and the elements beat time."

Whereupon the entire orchestra with one accord applauded in honour of an idea whose extent they in no way understood; they stopped playing to applaud. On the day of the concert this introduction produced an almost indescribable effect of mingled stupor and awe. I was seated by the side of the drummer, who, laying hold of one of my arms and pressing it convulsively, could not help calling out at intervals—

"It is superb! It is sublime! It is awe-inspiring! It is enough to turn one's brain!"

With my other hand I tore at my hair, and, forgetting that it was my own work, longed to be able to exclaim—

"It is *monstrous*, colossal, horrible!"

Lastly, you know our heroic Greek scene— the verse, *Le monde entier*, did not produce half the effect of this awful passage. In truth, it was very badly played. Bloc, who was conducting, made a mistake in the opening movement, *Des sommets d'Olympe*, and in trying to extricate the orchestra from the blunder, he caused a momentary disorder among the violins which was within an ace of spoiling the whole performance. In spite of this, the effect was tolerably great, greater, perhaps, than you imagine. The hurried march of the Greek auxiliaries, and the exclamation, *Ils s'avancent,* were wonderfully dramatic. I do not stand upon ceremony with you, as you perceive, and I am telling you frankly what I think of my music.

An artist belonging to the Opera told one of his comrades, on the night of the rehearsal, that the effect of the *Francs Juges* was the most extraordinary thing he had ever heard in his life.

"Next to Beethoven, of course," replied the other.

"Next to nobody," was the answer. "I defy anybody to discover a more terrible idea than that."

The whole Opera was present at my concert, and after it was over there were endless embracings. Those who were most pleased were Habeneck, Dérivis, Adolphe Nourrit, Dabadie, Prévost, Mademoiselle Mori, Alexis Dupont, Schneitzoeffer, Hérold, Rigel, &c. Nothing was wanting to my success, not even the criticisms of MM. Panseron and Brugnières, who have discovered that my style is new, but bad, and that it is wrong to encourage such a method of composition.

Ah! my dear friend, send me an opera! Robin Hood! How can you expect me to do anything without a poem? Write something, I beg of you.

Good-bye, my dear Ferrand. I send you weapons wherewith to oppose my detractors. Castil-Blaze was unable to be present at my concert owing to his absence from Paris. I saw him afterwards, and he promised to say something about it. He is not hurrying himself, but fortunately I can do without him, and that easily.

I only learnt yesterday that the article which appeared in the *Voleur*, which spoke of me more favourably than any of the others, is by Despréaux, who competed against me at the Institut; this testimony at the hands of a rival has flattered me considerably.

IV.

JUNE 28, 1828.

Oh, my friend, what a long time your letter has been in reaching me! I feared that mine had gone astray.

Echo has answered faithfully—

Yes, we understand each other fully, we feel alike; life is not altogether destitute of charm. Although I have, during the last nine months, led a poisoned, disillusioned existence, which my music alone has rendered me capable of supporting, your friendship is a connecting chain whose links grow closer and closer day by day while others break. (Do not indulge in conjectures; you would be mistaken.) I will do my utmost to spend a few days at Côte in about six weeks' time; as soon as my departure is settled, I will let you know and appoint a meeting at my father's house.

I am waiting very impatiently for the first and third acts of the *Francs Juges*, and I swear to you, on my honour, that I will send you a copy of the full score of the *Resurrexit*, and one of the *Mélodie*. I am having them copied as expeditiously as possible, and I will send them to you as soon as ever I get hold of them.

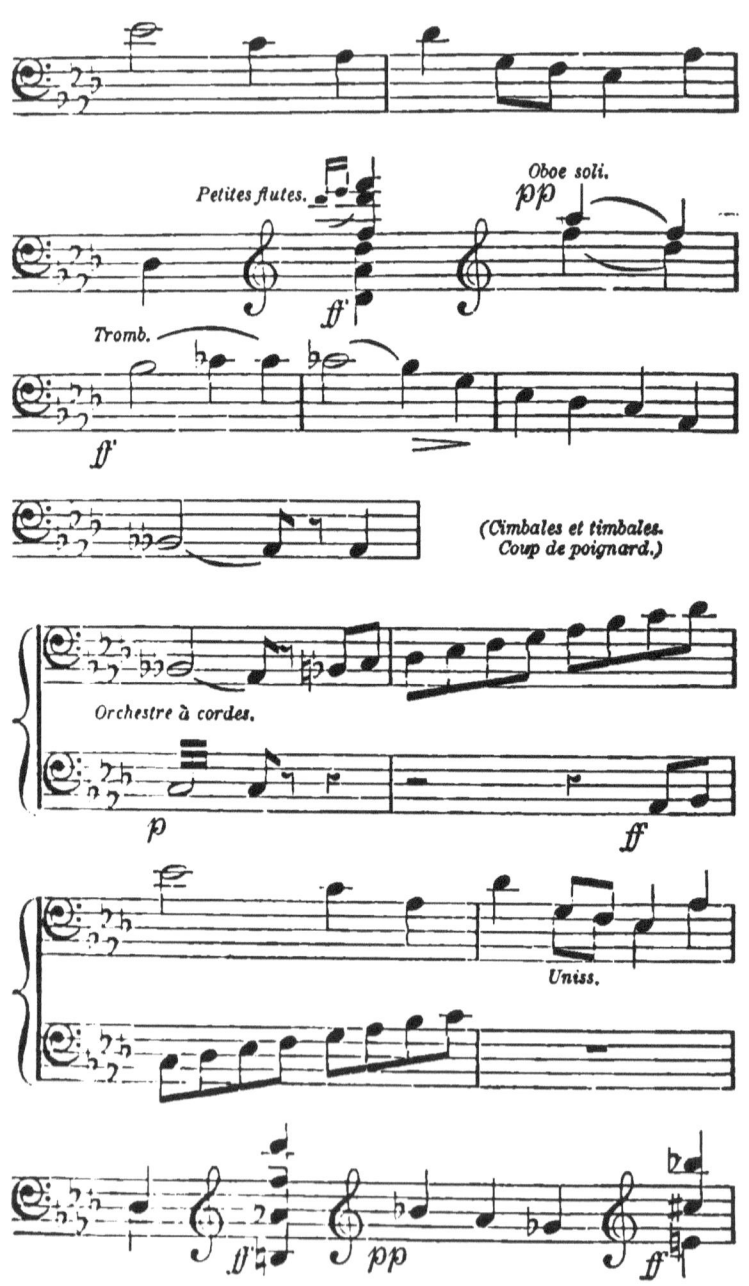

The allocution you mention is by an artist of
your acquaintance, Turbri, and fully justifies
the opinion you express about it. As you have
to see Duboys, you should tell him of the conversation I had the day before yesterday with
Paston, his old music-master. I met him in
the Rue Richelieu, and without giving me time
to say " How d'ye do," he said,

" Ah! I am right glad to see you. I went to
hear you. Are you aware of one thing—that
you are the Byron of music? Your overture
to the *Francs Juges* is a *Childe Harold*, and,
more than that, you are a master of harmony.
The conversation turned upon you the other
day at a dinner, and a young man who was
present said that he knew you, and that you
were a good fellow.

" ' What the devil does it matter,' I said to
him, ' whether he is a good fellow or the devil,
so long as he writes music like that. It's all
one to me ! ' I never thought, when you and I
applauded Beethoven together so enthusiasti-
cally, that a month later, on the same platform
and in the same room, you would be the one to
make me experience similar sensations. Good-
bye, my dear fellow, I am very pleased to know
you."

Can you imagine such an idiot?

A short time ago I found myself dining at the
same table with the youngest Tolbecque, the
fashionable one of the three. When he heard
my projected concert mentioned, he considered
it the height of conceit, and came to the conclusion that it would be undoubtedly depressing.
Well, in spite of that he played in my
orchestra, and the overture effected such a
revolution in him that, to use his own words,
" I turned as pale as death, and had no strength
to applaud effects which stirred my very soul;.
truly, it assures the success of the whole
piece."

Bringing these insignificant fellows to their·
bearings is a singular consolation to me.

I have several things in train at the present
moment, but nothing definite. Two operas are
in preparation for Feydeau, one for the Opera,.
and I am now going to call upon M. Laurent,
Director of the English and Italian theatres.
It is a question of arranging the English
tragedy, *Virginius*, for the Italian Opera. As
soon as I know anything definite, I will write
to you.

V.

JUNE 28, EIGHT HOURS LATER.

I have returned, not from M. Laurent, but
from Villeneuve-Saint-Georges, four leagues

from Paris, whither I went for a walk. It has
not killed me, in proof of which I am writing
to you. How lonely I am! All my muscles
are trembling as if I were on the point of
death. Oh! my friend, send me some work or
other—throw me a bone to gnaw. How lovely
the country is; how all-pervading the light!
Every living thing I met on my way back
seemed to be happy. The trees sighed sweetly,
and I was alone in that vast plain. Space, re-
moteness, the sense of being forgotten, grief
and rage surrounded me. In spite of all my
efforts, life escapes me, I am holding on to it
by a single thread.

At my age and with my temperament, to
possess nothing but distracting sensations—and
with all this, the persecutions of my family
are beginning again. My father sends me
nothing now, and my sister writes to say that
he will persist in his resolution. Money—
always money—yes, money brings happiness.
If I had enough, I might be happy, and death
is not happiness, so much is there wanting in it.

Neither during life—nor afterwards—nor before? When then? Never! Inflexible necessity!

And still the blood courses through my veins,

and my heart beats as if it were jumping for joy.

In fact, I am in wild spirits—joy, by heaven, joy!

VI.

SUNDAY MORNING.

MY DEAR FRIEND,

Do not distress yourself about these wretched aberrations of my heart; the crisis is past; I do not care about explaining the cause of them in a letter, because it might go astray. I insist upon your not saying a word about my state to anybody; a word even is so easily repeated, and if one reached the ears of my father he would not know a moment's peace. No one can do anything for me, and all that I can do is to suffer patiently until time, which changes so many things, shall change my destiny too.

Be prudent, I beseech you; be careful not to say a word to Duboys, because he might repeat it to Casimir Faure, and from him my father would hear it.

That frightful walk yesterday has undone me; I cannot move, all my joints are paining me, and yet I must walk the whole day long.

VII.

Paris, August 29, 1828.

My Dear Ferrand,

I leave to-morrow for Côte. At last I shall see my relatives once more after a separation of three years, and I imagine that nothing will prevent your fulfilling your promise, and that I shall have the pleasure of seeing you in the course of next month. I shall not stay beyond the 26th of September at the latest, so arrange to come to Côte as soon as you can. But write to me a week beforehand, because, if you do not give me due notice, I may be at Grenoble.

Auguste, who is now at Blois, has promised faithfully to meet me at Côte. I am going to write to him to arrange with you so that you can travel together from Belley or Lyon. I hope he will be able to manage it, and that you will both arrive at the same time. I am bringing you the two pieces you are waiting for; I could not give them to young Daudert because the copying of them was not finished. Good-bye; I count upon getting a letter from you on the 8th or 10th of September. Do not fail me.

VIII.

GRENOBLE, MONDAY, SEPTEMBER 16, 1828.

MY DEAR FRIEND,

I start to-morrow morning for Côte, from which place I have been absent since the day your letter arrived. It is impossible for me to pay you a visit. I must leave on the 27th inst., and I cannot even mention any further absence to my relations. I have already spoken of you to my family; they fully expected to see you, and your letter redoubled their impatience to meet you. This desire, on the part of my sisters and our young ladies, is somewhat interested; it is a question of balls and picnics in the country. Amiable cavaliers are in request, the species not being a common one here, and though perhaps all this fuss is being made on my account, I am not in the least adapted to contribute either animation or gaiety. I saw Casimir Faure the other day at my father's house; he is staying with his father in the country, and we are only separated by a distance negotiable in a couple of hours. Robert has come with me, and is the adored minstrel of all these ladies. Come as soon as you can, I beseech you; your music awaits you.

We will read *Hamlet* and *Faust* together,

Shakespeare and Goethe! the mute confidants of my woes, the interpreters of my life. Come come! Nobody here understands the rage of genius. The sun blinds them to it, and makes them regard it as eccentricity. Yesterday, when out driving, I composed the ballad of the *Roi de Thulé* in Gothic style; I will give it you for your *Faust* if you have not one already. Good-bye; time and space divide us; may we be reunited before our separation becomes further protracted. But let us quit that subject.

"Horatio, you are the man whose society has suited me best." I suffer much. It would be cruel of you not to come.

But you will come. Good-bye.

To-morrow I shall be at Côte. The day after, Wednesday, I shall have to help my family to entertain M. de Ranville, the Procureur-Général, who is coming with my uncle to spend a couple of days at home. On the 27th I take my departure; next week there is to be a grand *réunion* at the house of Hippolyte Rocher's cousin, pretty Mademoiselle Veyron.

IX.

PARIS, NOVEMBER 11, 1828.

MY DEAR FRIEND,

I thank you for your kindness, and I am only ashamed of not having done so before, but when I sent you the works you wanted, I was so ill and incapable of exertion that I pre-ferred to wait a few days before writing to you.

La Fontaine was quite right when he said, "Absence is the greatest of all evils." She has gone! She has been at Bordeaux for the last fortnight. I live no more, or, rather, I live too much, but I suffer the impossible, and I have scarcely courage to perform my new functions. You know that I have been appointed first Commissary of the Société du Gymnase-Lyrique. I am charged with the choice and replacing of the musicians, the hiring of the instruments, and the custody of the score and orchestral parts. It takes up all my time just now. Subscribers are coming in, and we have already two thousand two hundred francs in the treasury. The envious write anonymous letters; Cherubini is considering whether he shall be for us or against us; everybody is brawling at the Opera, and we continue steadily on our course. I am not having anything copied, as I am awaiting your letter.

You ask me how much it will cost to stereotype our Greek scene. It is a long time since I inquired about the cost of lithographing, but in France it costs a third more than printing. The stereotyped sheets of our work will mount up to seven hundred and fifty francs, and we should have fifty copies.

I have not yet met the author of *Atala* again; he is in the country. When I see him I will mention your *Scène* to him.

If you see Auguste, make my excuses for not having written to him, and tell him that I am surprised at not having yet heard of his trip to Côte. He told me, when I left, that he would pay my father a visit.

I met Flayol yesterday at the English lecture; he sent all sorts of messages to you.

X.

THE END OF 1828.

My Dear Friend,

I am answering you at once. I am very far from giving up our opera, and if I have not mentioned it to you, it has been because I did not want to bother you, and I was, moreover, under the impression that you were fully aware of how impatiently I await it. So finish it as soon as possible.

I am hard at work now for M. Choron's concerts; he has asked me for an oratorio for two solo voices, with organ accompaniment. I have already completed half of it, and I think it will be performed in about six weeks from now;

it will make me better known in the Faubourg Saint-Germain.

Do you know M. d'Eckstein sufficiently well to give me a letter of introduction to him? I have been told that he is on the staff of a large monthly paper,* the head of which is M. Beuchon, one of the editors of the *Constitutionnel.* This paper is to appear shortly; it is conceived on a grand scale, and the arts will occupy a foremost place in it. If I could inspire him with sufficient confidence in me, I would undertake the editorship of the musical articles; see if you can assist me in this. Should M. d'Eckstein present me, I presume that I should be accepted, or, at all events, they might try me.

Do you still suffer from your teeth? I send you as a New Year's gift a sublime air from *Vestale;* you do not know it because it has been suppressed for more than ten years. You appear to me to be sad; you want a good cry, and I make you a present of the air as a specific. In addition, I send you another air from *Fernand Cortez,* which is unknown to you for a similar reason; it is perhaps the finest in the whole composition.

YOUR FRIEND FOR LIFE.

* *Le Correspondant.*

XI.

PARIS, FEBRUARY 2, 1829.

I have been waiting all this time, my dear and excellent friend, in order with this letter to send you the complete score of my *Faust*, but as the work has assumed greater dimensions than I foresaw, the printing is not yet finished, and I cannot do any longer without writing to you.

Three days ago I was for twelve hours in a fearful delirium of joy. Ophelia is not so far away from me as I imagined; there exists some reason or other about which I am not to be told for some time to come, and it is consequently impossible at present to speak openly of it.

"But," she has said, "*if he loves me truly*, if his love is unlike the love of those whom I have every right to despise, a few months' waiting will not tire out his constancy."

If I love her truly! Turner knows plenty of other things, no doubt, but he persists in swearing to me that he knows nothing; I should not have even known so much if I had not wrested a part of my secret from his wife. I merely perceived that for some time past he has been speaking of my affairs more confidently and with a smiling air. One day he could not help

emerging from his English stolidity, and saying
to me :

"I shall succeed, I tell you; I am certain of
it.   If I go with her to Holland, I am sure of
having excellent news for you in a very short
time."

Well, my dear friend, he is to start with her
and her mother four days hence; he is entrusted with their French correspondence and
their pecuniary interests in Amsterdam.

She it is—it is Ophelia who has arranged all
this, and has desired it ardently.   *Ergo*, she
wants to talk to him about me much and often,
a thing she has hitherto been unable to do
owing to the continual presence of her mother
before whom she trembles like a child.

Listen to what I say, Ferrand; if ever I succeed, I feel beyond a doubt that I shall become a colossus in music; for some time past I
have had a descriptive symphony of *Faust* in my
brain; when I set it at liberty, I want to
astound the whole musical world with it.

The love of Ophelia has increased my abilities
a hundredfold.   Send me the *Francs Juges* as
soon as you can, in order that I may profit by a
moment's sun and quiet to ensure their reception ; darkness and storm come to prevent my
onward progress only too often ; it is absolutely

necessary that I should work now. I count on
your punctuality and I hope to receive your
poem before ten days have passed over my head.
A short time ago I received a letter from my
eldest sister, in reply to a lengthy epistle from
me, in which I frankly explained all my projects
about marriage, of course without saying that
my choice was made. Nancy replied that my
parents had read my letter (which was just what
I wanted), and from what she says, I gather
that they expected some such communication,
and were not in the least surprised; so that,
when the time comes for me to ask their consent, I expect the disturbance will be very
slight. I am going to send her my score to
Amsterdam. I have only just put my initials
on it. What if I should attain to being loved
by Ophelia, or, at least, if my love should flatter
her and be pleasing to her? My heart swells
high and my imagination in vain makes super-
human efforts to comprehend the immensity of
such happiness. What if I should live? Should
write? Should expand my wings? Oh! my dear
friend. Oh! my heart! Oh! love, love! All!
All!

Do not let my ecstasy alarm you; it is not so
blind as you may fear; misfortune has made me
defiant; I look straight before me, and I see

nothing certain; I tremble as much with fear as with hope.

We must wait for time; nothing stops that, so we may rely upon it.

Good-bye; send me the *Francs Juges* quickly, I beseech you.

Have you read *Les Orientales* of Victor Hugo? There are countless sublime thoughts in it. I have set his *Chanson des Pirates* to music with a tempest accompaniment. If I write it out fairly, and have time to make a copy, I will send it to you with *Faust*. It is the music of the sea-rover, the corsair, the brigand, the rough and savage-voiced filibuster; but I need not explain it to you, because you understand poetic music as well as I do.

XII.

FEBRUARY 18, 1829.

MY DEAR FRIEND,

I wrote to M. Bailly immediately on the receipt of your letter, but he has not answered me. Duboys, who has been here for some days, saw Carné the day before yesterday. They had some conversation about the newspaper,* and Carné said they relied upon me.

I called upon Carné about three weeks ago,

* *Le Correspondant.*

and he promised to write to me when anything definite should be decided on. I have not
heard a word from him since, and I do not
understand it at all.

As for the *Stabat* business, it stands thus :—
I mentioned it to Maresco, who had just returned to Paris, and he undertook to print it,
on condition of a guaranteed sale of at least
fifteen copies. The market price of the work
will be four francs and a half, and the fifteen
copies will be sold at two francs.

After what you told me of the number of
people who were inquiring about it from M.
Dupart, I did not hesitate to guarantee the disposal of the fifteen copies, and Maresco came
for the manuscript yesterday. It will be published before Holy Week, so that it can be sung
from the copies which I will send you.

As for the other subject, *her* atmosphere of
hope is not clouded over ; on the contrary. She
has not started yet, but will probably leave
Paris next Friday.

What a singular destiny is that of a lover
whose most ardent wish is the absence of her
he loves !

So long as she remains here I cannot obtain
any definite reply, but I am assured of a few
lines from her in answer to my letter which will

be handed to her at Amsterdam. Oh, God!
What will she say to me?

" Farewell, my dear, farewell; love ever your
friend."

XIII.

PARIS, APRIL 9, 1829.

I have not written to you, my poor, dear
friend, because I was incapable of writing. All
my hopes were so many frightful illusions. She
has gone, and on her departure, without one
spark of pity for the anguish of which she was
a witness on two successive days, she merely
left this message to be conveyed to me, " There
is nothing more impossible."

Do not ask me, my dear friend, to describe to
you in detail all that has happened to me during
these two fatal weeks; an accident befell me
the day before yesterday, which renders it impossible for me to write to you now upon that
subject; I am not yet sufficiently recovered. I
will endeavour to find a spare moment after I
have regained sufficient strength to remove the
barb which still remains in the wound.

I send you *Faust*, dedicated to M. de la Roche-
foucauld; it was not for his sake! If you can,
without inconvenience, lend me another hundred
francs to pay the printer, you will oblige me. I

would rather be indebted to you than to these people here, but I confess that if you had not offered them to me I should not have had the courage to ask you.

A thousand thanks for your opera, which Gonnet is copying for me at this moment; we are going to employ all our resources to ensure a favourable reception for it. It is superb; there are some sublime passages in it. You are a poet indeed! The *finale* of the Bohemians in the first act is a masterpiece; in my opinion, it will be the most original and best-written *libretto* ever produced; it is, I repeat, magnificent.

Do not be angry with me for leaving you so quickly. I am going to the post with my music. It is two o'clock already and I am in such suffering that I shall go to bed again when I get back.

She has been absent for thirty-six days, each one twenty-four hours long, and *there is nothing more impossible.*

I asked both Schott and Schlesinger, who deal in sacred music, whether they would let me have what you asked me for, but everything they have is on too large a scale.

I have written a *Salutaris* for three voices with organ accompaniment. I have been look-

ing for it all day long, for the purpose of sending it to you, but I have not been able to find
it. As it was not worth much I may very likely
have burnt it this winter.

XIV.

Paris, June 3, 1829.

My Dear Friend,

It will soon be three months since I
heard from you; I intended to wait still longer,
thinking that you might possibly be travelling,
but it appears that you have not left Belley, as
my sister wrote a day or two ago to say that you
had sent her some Swiss airs, for which she
asks me to thank you. Something extraordinary must, therefore, necessarily have happened.

I sent you *Faust* together with the copies of
the *Stabat* without any title-page; you have not
acknowledged their receipt, and I am at a loss to
understand it. Is there some fresh anonymous
quarrel? Does your father intercept our correspondence? Or are you perchance attaching
credence to the absurd calumnies which are cur-
rent about me among your family?

I did not send you the title-pages of the
Stabat; Maresco has left for the provinces and
I do not know where to lay hands on him.
Faust has had an immense success among the

artists; Onslow called upon me one morning and made me feel quite uncomfortable, so warmly did he praise it. Meyerbeer has just written to Schlesinger from Baden for a copy. Urhan, Chélard, and many of the most prominent artists of the opera have procured copies, and I receive fresh congratulations every night. But nothing has made such an impression upon me as the enthusiasm of Mr. Onslow. You know that, ever since the death of Beethoven, he has wielded the sceptre of instrumental music. Spontini has just produced his opera, the *Colporteur*, at Berlin, where it has met with a signal success. He is extremely difficult to please on the score of originality, and has assured me that he knows nothing more original than *Faust*.

" I am very fond of my own music," he added, " but I conscientiously believe that I am incapable of producing such a work."

To all this I could only answer trivialities, so upset was I by this unexpected visit. On the following day Onslow sent me a copy of the score of his two grand *quintetti*. Up to the present time this compliment has touched me more nearly than any other.

I have paid the printer what I owed him, a pupil having come to my rescue.

I am still very happy, my life is as charming as ever; no sorrow, no despair, plenty of illusions, and to put the finishing stroke to my enchantment, the *Francs Juges* has been rejected by the jury of the opera.   M. Alexandre Duval, who read the poem to the Committee, told me that it was considered too long and obscure. The only scene which pleased everybody was that of the Bohemians; he himself thought the style very remarkable, and was of opinion that there is a *poetic future in store for the author.*

I am going to have it translated into German. I will finish the music and make an opera of it like *Der Freischütz*, half dialogue, half melodrama, and the rest music.   I will add four or five bits, such as the *finale* of the first act, the *quintette*, the air for Lénor, &c., &c.   I am told that Spohr is not jealous, but, on the contrary, is anxious to help young composers. Consequently if I gain the prize at the Institut, I will start at once for Cassel ; he is the director of the theatre there, and I may secure a hearing for the *Francs Juges.*   Whatever may be the final result of all this, I am none the less extremely sensible of the trouble which the work cost you, and I thank you for it a thousand times.   It pleases me mightily.   I am preparing a grand concert for the beginning of December, in which I shall produce *Faust* with two great overtures and some Irish melodies which are not printed. I have only completed one up to now; Gounet is keeping me waiting a long time for the rest.

The *Revue Musicale* has published a very good article on *Faust*. I have not put any announcement of it in the other papers.

I cannot undertake any important composition. When I am strong enough to work I copy out the parts for the future concert, and I have not much time to devote to that, owing to being constantly worried for newspaper articles. I am charged with the correspondence, nearly gratuitous, for the *Gazette Musicale de Berlin*. My letters are translated into German; the proprietor of the paper is in Paris now, and he bores me to death. One of my articles appeared in *Le Correspondant*, but as in my second I attacked the Italian school, M. de Carné wrote to me the day before yesterday to ask me to write another on a different subject. I am considered to have been a trifle hard upon the Italian school. The *Prostituée* evidently has some lovers even among religious folk.

I am preparing a bibliographical notice on Beethoven.

I am on the free list for the German performances; *Der Freischütz* and *Fidelio* gave me some new sensations, in spite of the detestable orchestra at the Italiens, to which public opinion is at length doing justice. The papers just at present are especially strong in their con-demnation of it.

I have been offered an introduction to Rossini, but, as you may well imagine, I declined. I am not fond of that Figaro, or, to speak more correctly, I hate him more and more every day. The absurd remarks he made about Weber in the lobby of the German theatre exasperated me; I regretted very much that I did not hear him, and had no opportunity of giving him a bit of my mind on the subject.

My poor Ferrand, I write you interminable digressions which have no interest whatever for you, and I am inclined to fear that my letters no longer possess the interest in your eyes that they formerly had. If some strange alteration had not taken place in you, would you have re-mained so long without replying to my letter which accompanied the parcel of music? You ought to have received it in Holy Week. You have not even sent me a friendly word since I told you that I was losing all the hopes with which I had been deluding myself. I am no farther advanced than I was on the first day; this passion will kill me; it has been so often said that hope alone can sustain love! I am a convincing proof to the contrary. Ordinary fire has need of air, but electricity burns in a vacuum. All the English newspapers are loud in praise and admiration of her genius. I remain obscure. When I have written an immense instrumental composition, such as I am meditating, I want above all things to have it performed in London, so that I may gain a brilliant success under her very eyes!

My dear friend, I can write no more; my pen is falling from my fingers through sheer weakness.

XV.

JUNE 15, 1829.

Yes, my dear friend, it is quite true that I did not hear from you until the 11th inst., and I cannot imagine what has become of your letters. You may possibly find out, but I doubt it.

I shall be delighted to be announced in the *Journal de Genève* if you can manage it. In writing about my work, *Faust*, do not, I beseech you, be led away by your feelings of friendship for me; nothing appears so strange to the calm reader as enthusiasm which is unintelligible to him. I do not know what to say

to you about the summary of articles you mention. Look at the one in the *Revue Musicale,*
and allude to each subject in detail; or, if that
is beyond the compass of the paper, lay more
stress on the *Premier Chœur,* the *Concert des
Sylphes,* the *Roi de Thulé,* and the *Serenade,*
especially on the double orchestra of the *Concert,* which has not been mentioned by the
Revue, and wind up with a few considerations
upon the melodic style and the innovations you
consider the best.

I am not having any announcement put in the
other papers, because I am momentarily expecting a reply from Goethe, who sent word that
he was going to write to me, but does not do so.
Heavens! how impatient I am to receive that
letter! I have been somewhat better during
the last two days. Last week I was seized with
a nervous depression so severe that I could
hardly move or dress myself in the morning. I
was recommended to take baths, but they did
me no good; I remained quite quiet, and youth
regained the upper hand. I cannot get used to
the impossible, and it is precisely because it is
impossible that I have so little life left in me.

Nevertheless, constant occupation is an absolute necessity in my case; I am writing a life
of Beethoven for *Le Correspondant.* I cannot

find a moment for composition; during the rest of my time I have to copy out parts. What a life !

XVI.

JULY 15, 1829.

MY DEAR FRIEND,

I answer you by return in compliance with your request. I received your two acts safely. I think the last one magnificent; the interrogatory is especially beautiful, and the *dénoûment* is twenty thousand times better than the one we agreed upon. The remarks I have to make refer solely to the division of the musical pieces, and the too frequent conjunction of similar sensations, which would produce a disagreeable monotony in the first act. But we will discuss that point at some future time.

You ought long ago to have received the music I have to send you, and I may as well tell you at once the reason of the delay. After my concert, my father took a new whim into his head, and cut off my allowance, the result being that I am too short of money to pay the thirty or forty francs which the copying of my two pieces would cost; I did not like to ask Auguste to lend me them because I owe him fifty already. I cannot copy them myself, seeing

that for the last fortnight I have been a prisoner at the Institut.   This wretched competition is an absolute necessity as far as I am
concerned, because it gives me money, and
nothing can be done without that vile metal.

Auri sacra fames quid non mortalia pectora cogis!

My father even declined to contribute to the
expense of my sojourn at the Institut; M.
Lesueur provided the necessary funds for that.
I will write to you as soon as I have any news
to communicate.   Young Daudert, who leaves
on the 12th of August, will take charge of the
music for you if I can manage to get it by that
time.   I am too disheartened to write any more.
I forgot to tell you that Gounet has finished
his second act.

Good-bye.   I am glad you have met Casimir
Faure.   *La Vestale* is to be given to-night for
the first time these seven months, and I cannot
go.   I should have had tickets from Madame
Dabadie, who has promised to sing my *scène*.

XVII.

August 21, 1829.

My Dear Friend,

At last I am sending you the music
for which you have been waiting so long; the
fault rests with me and my printer.   As for me,

the competition at the Institut is some excuse, and all my new sources of agitation, *the new pangs of my despised love,* are unfortunately only too sufficient a justification for my thinking of nothing else. Yes, my poor, dear friend, my heart is the centre of a horrible conflagration; it is a virgin forest encircled by lightning; every now and then the fire appears burnt out, but there comes a puff of wind, it blazes up again, and the moaning of the trees as they succumb to the flames reveals the dread power of the devastating scourge.

It is of no use entering into details with regard to the fresh shocks I have recently received, but everything is coming upon me at once. This absurd and shameful competition at the Institut has done me a severe injury as regards my parents. The judges, who are not the *Francs Juges,* do not wish, so they say, to encourage me in my mistaken course. Boïeldieu said to me—

" My dear friend, you had the prize in your grasp and you let it fall. I came with the firm conviction that you would carry it off, but when I heard your work——! How could you expect me to give a prize to a thing *of which I have not an idea ? I do not understand* one half of Beethoven, and you go farther than Beethoven!

How do you expect me to understand you ? You mock the difficulties of harmony by being lavish of modulation, and, as far as I am concerned, *I have never studied harmony, and have no experience of that branch of our art!* It is my fault, perhaps, but I do not like music which puzzles me."

"But, sir, if you wish me to write quiet music, you should not have fixed upon such a subject as Cleopatra—a hopeless queen who exposes herself to the bite of an asp and dies in convulsions ! "

"Grace can be infused into everything. But I am far from saying that your work is bad ; I merely say that I cannot understand it yet, and that I should have to hear it several times, performed by an orchestra."

"Have I refused to let you hear it ? "

"Besides, when I saw all your eccentric forms, and your hatred for everything that is known, I could not help telling my colleagues at the Institut that a young man who possessed such ideas, and wrote in such a style, must despise us in his heart of hearts. You are a volcanic being, my dear friend, and it does not do to write for oneself; all organizations are not cast in the same mould. But come and see me; do me this pleasure, and we will talk the matter over, for *I want to study you.*"

On the other hand, Auber took me on one side at the Opera, and after having told me almost the same thing, with the additional information that one ought to write *cantatas as one writes symphonies,* he added—

" You avoid the beaten track, but you need never fear writing platitudes. Consequently, the best advice I can give you is to endeavour to write flatly, and when you have achieved something which appears horribly flat to you, it will be exactly what it ought to be. And do not forget that if you were to write music in accordance with your own conceptions, the public mind would not understand you, and the music sellers would not buy your works."

But, once for all, when I take it into my head to write for butchers and bakers, I shall not choose as my text the passions of the Queen of Egypt and her meditations upon her death. Oh, my dear Ferrand, I wish I could make you hear the scene where Cleopatra reflects upon the *greeting her shade will receive from those of the Pharaohs entombed in the Pyramids.* It is terrible, frightful! It is the scene where Juliet meditates on her entombment in the vaults of the Capulets, surrounded, while yet living, by the bones of her ancestors and the corpse of Tybalt —the dread which is ever increasing—reflec-

tions which end in cries of horror accompanied
by an orchestra of basses playing this rhythm—

In the midst of all this, my father stops my
indispensable allowance.   I am going back
to Côte, where I foresee no end of worry.
And yet, I only live for music; it alone supports me in this abyss of ills of every description.   Well, I must go there, and you *must*
come and see me; remember how rarely we
meet, how frail is my tenure of life, and how
near we are to each other!   I will write to you
immediately on my arrival.

Guillaume Tell?   I think all the journalists
have gone mad.   It is a work possessing a few
good numbers, which is not absurdly written,
in which there is no *crescendo* and rather less
big drum—that is all.   Beyond that, there is

no real feeling, but everywhere art, habit, *savoir-faire*, and the knowledge how to manage the public. And it goes on—everybody yawns, and the management gives away innumerable orders. Adolphe Nourrit as young *Melchtal* is sublime; Mademoiselle Taglioni is not a dancer, she is a spirit of the air, Ariel personified, a daughter of the skies. And people have the audacity to place this above Spontini! I had a talk on that subject in the orchestra the day before yesterday with M. de Jouy. They were doing *Fernan Cortez*, and although he is the author of the *libretto* of *Guillaume Tell,* he spoke of Spontini as we do, with adoration. He, Spontini, is continually coming back to Paris; he has had a quarrel with the King of Prussia, and his ambition has ruined him. He has just produced a German opera which fell flat; the success achieved by Rossini drives him mad, which is quite intelligible, but he ought to rise above the infatuation of the public. The composer of *La Vestale* and *Cortez* writing for the public! People who applauded the *Siège de Corinth* come and tell me that they *love* Spontini, and he seeks after such encomiums! He is very miserable; the failure of his last work is killing him.

I am composing some Irish melodies to

Moore's words, which Gounet is translating for me; I finished one a few days ago, and am delighted with it. One of these days an opera is to be brought out for me at Feydeau; I am very much pleased about it. May it be received!

You are always promising me something and never performing anything; nevertheless, we are on the eve of a theatrical revolution which will be favourable to us; do not forget that. The Porte-Saint-Martin is ruined, the Nouveautés is in the same case, and the managers of these theatres are stretching out their arms to music. It is probable that the Ministry will sanction a new operatic theatre; I mention this because I know it.

XVIII.

OCTOBER 3, 1829.

MY DEAR FERRAND,

I send you a few lines in great haste. Hostilities have recommenced. I give a concert on the 1st of November, All Saints' Day. I have already secured the Menus-Plaisirs concert room; Cherubini, instead of opposing me this time, is ill. I shall give two grand overtures, *Le Concert des Sylphes*, and the *Grand Air de Conrad*, to which I have added an accompanied recitative, and have improved

the instrumentation.   Madame J. Dabadie
promised me yesterday that she would sing.
Hiller is to play a pianoforte *concerto* by Beethoven, which has never been performed in Paris.
Sublime ! Immense!

Mademoiselle Heinefetter, whose success at
the Italian Opera you must have seen in the
newspapers, will sing the *scena* from *Der
Freyschütz* in German.   At all events, she would
like nothing better, and the consent of the
Manager, M. Laurent, is alone wanting.
Habeneck is to conduct my orchestra, which,
as you may well imagine, will be astounding.

Shall it be said that you are never to hear
me ? Come, then, to Paris, if only for a
week.

I have not been able to go to Côte. I have
so much running about, and so much copying to
do, that I must leave you already, but write
to me as soon as you can, I beseech you. Above
all, assure me that you will make some excuse
to your father to allow of your being here on
All Saints' Day.

Meyerbeer has just arrived from Vienna; on
the day following his arrival, he sent a message
by Schlesinger to compliment me upon *Faust*.

A musical paper has devoted an article of
three columns to me. If I can get a copy of it,
I will send it you.

Farewell, we may meet again I trust.   Come,
come then ; 'tis not so long.

XIX.

FRIDAY EVENING, OCTOBER 30, 1829.

Oh, Ferrand, Ferrand, my friend, where are
you?   This morning we had the first rehearsal
of the *Francs Juges.*   Forty-two violins, and a
total of a hundred and ten performers!   I am
writing to you from the Lemardelay *restaurant*
while I am waiting for my dessert.   Nothing, I
swear to you, nothing is so terrifically fearful
as my overture to the *Francs Juges.*   Oh,
Ferrand, my dear friend, you would understand
me ; where are you?   It is a hymn to despair,
the most deplorable, horrible, tender despair
that can be imagined.   Habeneck, who conducted my immense orchestra, was really afraid
of his task.   They had never seen anything so
difficult, but, apparently, they did not think ill
of it, for at the end of the overture they overwhelmed me, not only with frantic applause,
but also with sounds almost as terrifying as
those of my orchestra.   Oh, Ferrand, Ferrand,
why are you not here?

I am going to the Opera at once in search of
a harmonica ; they brought me one this morning which was too low, and we could not make
use of it.   The sextet out of *Faust* goes

splendidly, my very sylphs are enchanted. The overture of *Waverley* does not go well yet; we shall rehearse it again to-morrow, and it *shall* go. And the *Jugement Dernier*, as you know it, but with the addition of a recitative accompanied by four pairs of kettle-drums in harmony. Oh Ferrand, Ferrand, a hundred and twenty leagues!

Yesterday I was too ill to walk; to-day, the demons of the infernal regions, who dictated the *Francs Juges*, have given me incredible strength. This evening I must run all over Paris. The *concerto* by Beethoven is a prodigious, astounding, sublime conception! I do not know how to express my admiration.

Oh, the sylphs!

I have composed a *pianissimo* solo for the big drum in the *Francs Juges*.

Intonuere cavæ gemitumque dedere cavernæ.

In a word, it is terrible! All the fury and tenderness that my heart contains are in this overture.

Oh Ferrand!

XX.

PARIS, NOVEMBER 6, 1829.

MY DEAR FERRAND,

I ought to have sent you an account of my concert before this; ever since my last letter you have been, no doubt, boiling over with impatience for the details. But, first of all, are you quite well again? Has your indisposition entirely disappeared? Gounet has received a letter from Auguste, informing him of the unsatisfactory state of your health, and, indeed, what you yourself have told me makes me fear that it is still in somewhat the same condition.

However, since you take such a lively interest in whatever concerns me, and your friendship leads you to share all my anxieties so fully, I will tell you that my success was immense; the overture to the *Francs Juges* had an especial effect upon the audience, and drew forth four rounds of applause. Mademoiselle Marinoni had just gone forward to sing an Italian *pasquinade* and, taking advantage of the momentary lull, I was trying to slip between the music stands to fetch a roll of music left on one of the seats, when the audience perceived me; then the shouts and bravos recommenced, the performers joined in, a hail-storm of bows fell upon the violins, the violoncellos, and the stands, and I was very nearly overcome. Then followed embracings without end—but you were not there! As I was going out, after the crowd had dispersed, the performers waited for me in the courtyard of the Conservatoire, and as soon as I appeared the applause began again in the open air. In the evening at the Opéra it was the same thing over again—the orchestra and the lobbies in a state of ferment. Oh my friend, why are you not here? I have been suffering from intense melancholy ever since Sunday; all this excess of emotion has upset me; my eyes are constantly full of tears, and I feel as if I should like to die.

As regards the receipts, they have covered the expenses, and left me a hundred and fifty francs to the good. I am going to hand two-thirds over to Gounet, who has been kind enough to lend me money, and who is, I fancy, more pressed for it than you are. As soon as I shall have succeeded in realizing a tolerably present-able sum, I will lose no time in arranging for its transmission to you, for I am worried about being in your debt for so long.

At present the *Figaro* and the *Débats* are the only papers which have alluded to my concert. Castil-Blaze does not enter into any details; these beasts can only talk when there is nothing to say. I will send you all the papers which may mention me.

Good-bye; get well quickly and write to me.

XXI.

PARIS, DECEMBER 4, 1829.

MY DEAR FERRAND,

I have not received any reply to my two letters or to the batch of newspapers I sent you in connection with my concert. You are ill, that is certain; have you no means of letting me hear of you, and relieving me from the mental anxiety from which I have been suffering for so long?

A letter which Gounet has received from Auguste says nothing cheering about your health.

Write to me, I beseech you, if it is only a line or two, or else get somebody to write for you. I will send you shortly some new compositions which I have just had printed. I am all expectation.

XXII.

PARIS, DECEMBER 27, 1829.

MY DEAR FERRAND,

Business first. I saw M. Rocher on the evening of the day I received your letter. With regard to Germain, he told me that there had been a judge-auditorship vacant at Lyons, but

that it had just been filled up. There is consequently no hope.

Congratulations next. I congratulate you a
thousand times, in my turn, on the brilliant
success you have had. I am not at all at a loss
to imagine the impression you must have produced, animated as you were by indignation and
the interest with which your client inspires
you. Once more, embrace that most excellent
Auguste for me; I am rejoiced for his sake at
this stroke of luck. Gounet is sending him
hearty congratulations on the same subject.
Tell him that if I have not written to him, it is
because—because—I am an idle fellow who is,
nevertheless, always thinking of him with the
most sincere affection.

Reproaches now. You are beyond all forgive-
ness for having left me so long in anxiety. I
wrote to you three times, and you reply six
weeks after my third letter. I imagined you
were still ill. Then I thought that my letters
might possibly have been intercepted. I sent
you the newspapers; they have miscarried. If
you make a point of it, I will send you the
copies I have, on condition that you send them
back to me after you have read them. I may
want them.

Now for promises. You will receive, between

now and three weeks hence, our collection of
Mélodies Irlandaises, together with the *Ballet
des Ombres* which Dubois asked me to write,
and which is already printed.   I have attempted
to set one of the couplets of your satanic song
to music.   It is passable, but it will not stand
by the side of the others.   It is a horribly
difficult thing to do.   You are too much a poet
to suit a musician.   I do not know whether I
shall succeed.   In any case, your poem is admirable in its terrible truth, and it is full of bold
and novel expressions.

Finally, a confession.   I am weary, I am
weary !   The same thing over and over again.
But I grow weary now with astonishing rapidity,
and I get through as much weariness now in
an hour as I used to do in a day, and I drink
time as ducks do water, for the purpose of finding something to live upon, and, like them, I
only find a few uncouth insects.   What am I to
do ?   What am I to do ?

Good-bye ; at all events, answer both my
letters.

XXIII.

PARIS, JANUARY 2, 1830.

I wrote to you a week ago; your letter, just
received, makes no mention of mine; it is possible that the bad state of the roads, by delay-

ing the post, have caused our letters to cross. God grant that it, too, is not lost!

No, I have never heard of the thirty-five francs you sent me from Lyon. I told you so in one of the three letters I wrote to you after my concert, but as you displayed neither uneasiness nor astonishment in your tardy reply, I thought that the letter in which I mentioned the circumstances had not reached you. I should have sent Maresco the thirty-five francs which M. Dupart owes him long ago, but the fact is, that since I have been having my music stereotyped I have never had any available surplus. When at length you wrote to me six weeks ago to tell me that you had sent me from Lyon a draft for thirty-five francs, I replied that I had not received it, and that I was waiting to know what had become of it. I was never more surprised than I was when I noticed the absence of any allusion to the matter in your last letter.

To sum up—you sent me on one occasion
   the manuscript of the *Francs Juges* .   LOST.
On another occasion, a draft for thirty-
   five francs . . . . . .   LOST.
I sent you a packet of newspapers, postage prepaid, and put into the post by
   myself . . . . . .   LOST.

You wrote to me, telling me not to reply,
four days before your last visit to Paris ;
if you had not told me so, I should
have known nothing about it   .   .   LOST.
I wrote you the famous letter whose fate
has been such a cause of anxiety to
us   .   .   .   .   LOST.
I wrote to you three times after my concert, and informed you, I believe, in
my second letter that I had not received
Marescot's money; to-day I hear from
you that you know that, but you do
not get the information from me ; consequently, that letter has also been   .   LOST.

My dear friend, there is something extraordinary about all this, which it behoves us to
clear up.

Marescot has set out for the provinces ; I met
him at my printer's, and he told me that he was
going to write to M. Dupart for his money.
Even if he were here, I should be unable to let
him have it, seeing that at this moment I am
possessed of only twenty francs, and my allowance has been paid. In a day or two I ought
to receive from Troupenas two hundred francs
for some corrections I am making for him in
Guillaume Tell. I am always in the same state,
a thousand times poorer than a painter. All

told, I have only ten pupils, who bring me in forty-four francs a month.   My father sends me money from time to time, but when I have arranged matters so as to leave myself tolerably comfortable, his commissions, which have nearly always to be paid for, arrive on the scene, and that upsets all my economy.   I am in your debt, and I still owe Gounet more than a hundred francs; this is a perpetual worry to me, and the thought of these debts, although they are owing to tried friends, torments me incessantly.   On the other hand, your father persists in brooding over the absurd idea that I am a gambler—I, who have never touched a card nor set foot in a gaming-house.   The thought that in the eyes of your parents our friendship is not the most advantageous thing in the world for you, makes me beside myself.

Do not send me your *Dernière Nuit de Faust*. If I had it in my hands I should not be able to resist it, and my plan of work is mapped out for a long time to come.   I have to complete an immense musical composition for my concert next year, in which you must help me. If I succeed with your brigand song, which I think sublime, you will not have long to wait. Our melodies are being stereotyped; as soon as they appear we will send them to you, which does

not imply that you will receive them. Some of
them, I expect, will please you. Gounet and I
are having them stereotyped at our own expense, and by this means we reckon upon saving
money in the end. Have you Hoffman's *Contes
Fantastiques?* They are very curious.

When shall we see you here? Write to me
more frequently, I beseech you of your cle--
mency.

XXIV.

PARIS, FEBRUARY 6, 1830.

MY DEAR FRIEND,

Your letter and the thirty-five francs
enclosed in it have reached me this time.
Marescot is not in Paris; as soon as he returns I will give them to him. I shudder
when I think how you must be suffering from
your teeth; if it is likely to be any consolation to you, I can tell you that I am very
nearly in the same state, and last month I
suffered the agonies of the damned! I tried
several spirituous waters; the *Paraguay-roux,*
of which I had heard good accounts, in a
couple of days completely took away a dreadful
pain caused by a hollow tooth. I filled the
hollow with saturated cotton wool, and rinsed
my mouth with water mixed with a few drops
of the specific. Try it, leave no stone unturned.

Alas! I have another ill of which, apparently, nothing will cure me except a specific against life.

After a period of calm, violently disturbed by the composition of the *Elégie en Prose* with which my *Mélodies* conclude, I have just been plunged once more into all the anguish of an interminable and inextinguishable passion, devoid of both motive and subject. She is still in London, and yet I seem to feel her near me; all my former feelings for her are aroused, and combine to tear me in pieces; I hear my heart beat, and its pulsations shake me as though they were the strokes of the piston-rod of a steam engine. Every nerve in my body trembles with pain. In vain! Frightful!

Unhappy woman! If she could realize for an instant all the poetry, all the infinity of such love, she would fly into my arms, even if death lurked in my embrace.

I was on the point of commencing my great symphony (*Episode de la Vie d'un Artiste*), wherein the development of my passion is to be pourtrayed; I have it all in my head, but I cannot write a line. Patience!

You will receive, simultaneously with this letter, two copies of my dear *Mélodies*. An artist belonging to the Italian Opera in London is going to present one to Moore, whom he knows, and to whom we have dedicated them. Adolphe Nourrit intends to sing them at the "at-homes" to which he is in the habit of going.

The great point now is to give them publicity, but I have no activity left.

My dear friend, write to me often and at length, I beseech you; I am separated from you; let your thoughts, at all events, reach me. I cannot bear not being able to see you. Is it a stern necessity that through the thunder clouds which mutter over my head no single ray of peaceful light should console me? I expect a letter from you in nine days' time if your health will permit of your writing.

XXV.

PARIS, APRIL 16, 1830.

MY DEAR FRIEND,

I have been a long time without writing to you, but I have also waited in vain for the letter you were to have sent me by Auguste on his return to Paris. Since my last, I have encountered some terrible storms, but the vessel that was almost shipwrecked has recovered herself at last, and now sails calmly on. The discovery of frightful, but indisputable, truths has aided my recovery, and I think it will be as complete as my tenacious nature will allow. I have just strengthened my resolution by a work with which I am perfectly satisfied, and of which this is the subject, to be set forth in a programme and distributed in the concert-room on the night of the performance—

Episode de la Vie d'un Artiste, a grand fantastic symphony in five parts.

First part, in two portions, composed of a short *adagio,* followed immediately by an *allegro* developed—flood of passions, aimless reveries, delirious passion with all the accessories of tenderness, jealousy, fury, fear, &c.

Second part: Scene in the fields, *adagio,* thoughts of love and hope troubled by dark presentiments.

Third part: A ball—music brilliant and inspiriting.

Fourth part: March to the scene of execution—music pompous and wild.

Fifth part: Vision of a night of revelry.

That is the present plan of my romance, or my history, the hero of which you will easily recognise.

For my subject I take an artist gifted with a lively imagination, finding himself in

that state of mind which Chateaubriand has
depicted so admirably in his *René*, beholding
for the first time a woman who realizes
the ideal of beauty and charm for which
his heart has long yearned, and falling
violently in love with her.   By an odd singu-
larity, the image of her he loves never presents
itself to his mind, unless accompanied by a
musical thought in which he discovers qualities of grace and nobility similar to those with
which he has endowed his beloved.   This double
and fixed idea haunts him incessantly, and it is
the reason of the constant appearance, in all the
parts of the symphony, of the principal melody
in the first *allegro* (No. 1).

After almost interminable agitation, he discovers some grounds for hope ; he believes himself beloved.   One day, when he is in the
country, he hears from afar two herdsmen singing a *ranz des vaches ;* this pastoral duet
plunges him into a delicious reverie (No. 2).
The melody reappears for an instant through
the themes of the *adagio*.

He is present at a ball, but the tumult of the
fête is powerless to distract him; his fixed idea
still comes to trouble him, and the cherished
melody makes his heart beat in the midst of a
brilliant waltz (No. 3).

In a fit of despair he poisons himself with opium, but, the narcotic, instead of killing him, produces a horrible dream, during which he imagines that he has killed her he loves, and that he is condemned to death and to witness his own execution. March to the scene of the execution; immense procession of executioners, soldiers, and people. At the end, the melody appears once more, like a last thought of love, interrupted by the fatal blow (No. 4).

He then beholds himself surrounded by a disgusting crowd of sorcerers and devils assembled to celebrate the night of revelry. They call him from afar. The melody, which up to this time has seemed full of grace, now appears under the guise of a trivial, ignoble, drunkard's song; it is his beloved coming to the revels, to assist at the funeral *cortége* of her victim. She is no longer anything but a courtesan worthy of figuring in such an orgie. The ceremony then commences. The bells toll, the infernal element prostrate themselves, a choir chants the *Dies Iræ*, which is taken up by two other choirs who parody it in a burlesque manner; finally, there is a whirl of revelry, and when it is at its height it mingles with the *Dies Iræ*, and the vision comes to an end (No. 5).

There you have the plan, already carried

out, of this stupendous symphony. I have
just written the last note. If I can contrive
to be ready by the day of Pentecost, the 30th
of May, I will give a concert at the Nouveautés with an orchestra of two hundred and
twenty performers. I fear I shall not have
the copies of the parts ready. At present I am
quite stupid. The fearful strain of thought to
which my work is due has fired my imagination, and I am continually wanting to sleep
and rest myself. But, if my brain slumbers,
my heart is awake, and I feel the want of you
keenly. Oh, my friend, shall I not see you
again?

XXVI.

Paris, May 13, 1830.

My Dear Friend,

Your cousin Eugène Daudert ought to·
have handed you a letter from me almost on the
day I received yours. I will not let Auguste go
without giving him another. He tells me that
he shall see you very soon after his arrival. Your
letter affected me excessively; your anxiety
about the danger you imagined I was running
in connection with Henrietta Smithson, the
outpourings of your heart, your advice! Ah,
my dear Humbert, it is indeed a rare thing to
find a complete man, who has a soul, a heart, and

imagination, so very rare a thing for ardent and impatient natures like ours to encounter, that I know not how to express to you my thoughts upon my happiness in knowing you.

I think you will be satisfied with the plan of my *Symphonie Fantastique*, which I sent you in my letter. The vengeance is not too severe. Moreover, I did not write the vision of a night of revelry in that spirit. I have no desire for vengeance. I pity and despise her. She is but an ordinary type of woman, endowed with an instinctive power of expressing those pangs of the human soul which she has never felt, and incapable of entertaining a grand and noble sentiment such as that with which I have honoured her.

To-day I am concluding my final arrangements with the managers of the Nouveautés for my concert on the 30th of this month. They are very straightforward and obliging; we shall begin the rehearsals of the *Symphonie Gigantesque* in three days; all the parts have been copied out with scrupulous care; there are two thousand three hundred pages of music, nearly four hundred francs' worth of copying. It is to be hoped that our receipts will be considerable, as all the theatres are closed on the day of Pentecost.

That wonderful singer, Haitzinger, is to take part in it, and I hope to secure Madame Schrœder-Devrient, who, with her rival, is enchanting the Salle Favart every other night in *Der Freischütz* and *Fidelio*.

A propos, Haitzinger asked me the other day if there was a good tenor part for him in our opera of the *Francs Juges*. Acting upon my reply, and upon what all the Germans of his acquaintance said about me, he insisted upon carrying off the *libretto*, with the vocal score without accompaniment, in order to have it translated, and he intends to give it in its new dress at his benefit, which is to take place at Carlsruhe this year. That will be charming; I have only to finish the finale, two or three airs for tenor and soprano, and a quintet. I shall start for Carlsruhe in a few months, preceded by a species of reputation made by Haitzinger and others.

I may tell you that you are almost at one with Onslow in your opinion about my *Mélodies*. He prefers the four following, the *Chanson à boire*, the *Elégie*, the *Réverie*, and the *Chant sacré*. My dear fellow, it is not so difficult as you imagine, but it needs a pianist. When I write for the piano, I write for people who know how to play, and not for amateurs who do not know even

how to read music.   The Misses Lesueur, who
are certainly not *virtuosi*, accompany the *Elégie
en Prose* very well, and it, with the *Chant Guerrier*, is the least easy.   Poor Mademoiselle
Eugénie, who has an unfortunate attachment
for an amiable, cold, and somewhat senseless
youth, was at first completely puzzled by this
piece.   She confessed to me that at the first on-
set she understood literally none of it, but, in
studying it, she discovered a thought; she recognised it in the mournful picture of a being
dying of love; now, it is a passion with her;
she is always playing the ninth *Mélodie.*   I have
never heard it sung yet; only Nourrit can do
that, and I doubt his consenting to rouse himself to the state of fearful excitement in which
he ought to be, if he would interpret those accents of a breaking heart.   He has my *Mélodies,* and one of these days I will ask him to
sing me that one.   Hiller shall accompany him,
and we three will be alone.   At my concert I
shall repeat the overture to the *Francs Juges* in
order to move the audience and make the ladies
sob; besides, it is a sure means of attracting
the world; it enjoys such a reputation at present that many people will come for it alone.

You alone will not come! My father even
wants to be present, so he wrote me the day be-

fore yesterday. But my symphony? I hope
that unhappy woman will be present; at all
events, several people at Feydeau are putting
their heads together to make her come. I,
however, do not believe she will; if she
reads the programme of my instrumental
drama, she cannot help recognising herself,
and from that moment she will take every
care not to appear. God only knows what
will be said, as so many people know my
history.

XXVII.

PARIS, JULY 24, 1830.

MY DEAR FRIEND,

I am thoroughly reassured on your
account. Imagine, three letters without a
single reply. You send me a few lines promising me whole pages to come; if you only
knew how many times I have come home
from a long distance merely to see if the letter,
so impatiently awaited, had at length arrived,
you would be really concerned at not having
kept your promise to me. How lazy you are!
for I hope you are not ill. I am still awaiting your letter. Fortunately, my dear friend,
everything is going on well.

All the tenderness and delicacy that love can
hold, I possess. My ravishing sylph, my Ariel,

my life, appears to love me more than ever. As
for me, her mother is incessantly repeating that
if she were to read in a novel the description of
a love like mine, she would not believe it. We
have been separated for a few days, as I have
been shut up in the Institut *for the last time.* I
must win the prize, for upon it depends our
happiness in a great measure ; like Don Carlos
in *Hernani,* I say, *Je l'aurai.* She torments herself by thinking of it continually. To give me
some comfort in my imprisonment, Madame
Mooke sends her maidservant to me every other
day with a message telling me how they are
going on, and asking for news of me. What
ecstasy when I see her again some ten or twelve
days hence ! We shall in all probability have
many obstacles to overcome, but we shall con-
quer them. What do you think of all that ?
Can you imagine anything like it—such an
angel, and *the most striking talent in Europe !*
It has recently come to my knowledge that
M. de Noailles, in whom the mother has great
confidence, actually pleaded my cause, and was
strongly of opinion that, as her daughter loved
me, she should be given to me without so much
importance being attached to the monetary side
of the question. My dear fellow, if you only
heard her *thinking aloud* the sublime concep-

tions of Weber and Beethoven, you would lose your head. I have so strongly advised her not to play any *adagio* movements that I hope she will not often do so.   Such engrossing music kills her.   Of late she has been in such suffering that she thought she was going to die; she urged that I should be sent for, but her mother refused.   On the following day I saw her, pale and lying on a sofa.   How we wept! She was under the impression that she had something the matter with her chest.   I thought I should die with her, and I told her so ; she made no reply, but the idea was a source of infinite pleasure to me.   When she got well she reproached me for having entertained it.

"Do you think that God has given your musical organization for nothing ? You have no right to abandon the task confided to you ; I forbid you to follow me if I die."

But she will not die.   No, those eyes so full of genius, that slender figure, all that delicious being is more fit to wing its flight towards the skies than to lie withered beneath the humid ground.

Good-bye; I must work.   I am going to finish the instrumentation of the last air in my scene.   It is *Sardanapale*.   If you do not write, you will have to cry quits with a fifth letter from me. Spontini is here; I shall pay him a visit as soon as I get away from the Institut.

XXVIII.
PARIS, AUGUST 23, 1830.

You have left me for a very long time without any news of you. Something altogether out of the common is evidently necessary to induce you to take hold of a pen—but I will not reproach you.

The prize was awarded to me unanimously, the first time such a thing has been known. So the Institut is conquered. The noise of the salute and the *feu de joie* had a favourable effect upon my last piece, which I was at that time finishing.

Oh, my friend, what happiness it is to have achieved a victory which is a source of enchantment to a being beloved! My idolized Camille * was almost dead with anxiety when I brought her, last Thursday, the news so ardently longed for. Oh, my *delicate Ariel*, my sweet angel, your wings were all ruffled, but joy has given them back their lustre; even her mother, who looks upon our love with a certain amount of disfavour, could not help shedding tears of tenderness.

* Subsequently celebrated as a pianist under the name of Marie Pleyel.

I never suspected it; in order not to alarm me, she had persistently concealed the immense importance she attached to the prize, but now I can see what her real feeling was with regard to it.

"The world," she said to me, "the world looks upon it as a signal proof of talent; the world's mouth must be closed."

My *Scène* will be performed in public with full orchestra on the 2nd of October; my sweet Camille will be there with her mother; she never ceases talking about it. This ceremony, which without her would be childish in my eyes, will become an intoxicating *fête*. You will not be there, my dear, my very dear friend. You have only seen my tears of bitterness; when will you see my eyes glisten with those of joy!

There will be a concert at the Théâtre-Italien on the 1st of November. The new conductor of the orchestra, whom I know privately, has asked me to compose an overture for that day. I am going to write him an overture to *The Tempest* of Shakespeare, for piano, chorus and orchestra. It will be a new style of piece. On the 14th of November I shall give my monster concert, for the production of my *Symphonie Fantastique*, of which I sent you a programme. In the course of the winter the Concert Society will perform my overture to the *Francs Juges*; I have their positive promise. But I must achieve a success at the theatre; my happiness depends upon it. Camille's parents cannot give their consent to our marriage until that has been accomplished. Circumstances will be in my favour, I hope. I do not want to go to Italy, and I shall ask the King to dispense with that ridiculous journey in my case, and to grant me the allowance in Paris. As soon as I have realized a tolerable sum, I will send you the amount you so good-naturedly lent me. Goodbye, my dear friend, write to me and do not mention politics; I need no effort to make me silent on that subject. I have just left Madame Mooke's house; I have just quitted the hand of my adored Camille, and that is the reason why mine shakes so, and I am writing so badly. She has, however, played neither Weber nor Beethoven to me to-day.

That wretched girl Smithson is still here. I have never set eyes upon her since my return.

XXIX.

OCTOBER, 1830.

Oh, my dear, my inexpressibly dear friend! I am writing to you from the Champs Elysées, in the corner of an arbour exposed to

the setting sun. I see its golden rays glisten-
ing upon the dead or dying leaves of the
young trees which surround my retreat. I
have been talking about you all day to one who
understands, or rather divines, your soul. I am
irresistibly impelled to write to you. What are
you doing? You are eating away your heart,
I would wager, by reason of misfortunes which
only affect you in imagination; there are so
many which touch us nearly, that it grieves
me to see you succumb under the weight of
sorrow to which you are a stranger, or from
which you are far removed. Why? Why? I
understand it better than you imagine; it is
your existence, your poetry, your *Chateau-
brianisme*.

I suffer strangely from not seeing you;
chained down as I am, I am powerless to anni-
hilate the space which divides us. And yet
I have so much to say to you. If any good
fortune which falls to my lot can serve to win
you from your sombre thoughts, I can tell you.
that my music is to be performed at the Opèra
in the course of this month. To my adored
Camille once more I owe this honour. And
this is how it came about.

In her slender form, her capricious flight,
her distracting grace, and her musical genius,

I recognised the *Ariel* of Shakespeare. My poetic ideas, attracted by the drama of *The Tempest,* have inspired me with a gigantic overture, in an entirely novel style, for orchestra, chorus, two pianos (each four hands), and HARMONICA. I proposed it to the director of the Opéra, and he has undertaken to produce it at *a grand extraordinary performance.* My dear fellow, it is far grander than the overture to the *Francs Juges.* It is entirely new. With what profound adoration did I thank my idolized Camille for having inspired me with this composition! I told her a short time ago that my work was going to be performed, and she literally trembled with joy. I told her confidentially, whispered it in her ear, after two long kisses and an impassioned embrace, love, grand and poetic, as WE understand it. I am going to see her this evening. Her mother does not know that I am to be heard continually at the Opéra. We shall keep it from her until the last moment. You are a man under the sway of imagination, and you must, therefore, be a supremely unhappy one. So am I. We suit each other wonderfully. My friend, write to me at all events, since we cannot meet.

The coronation at the Institut will take place on the 30th of this month. *Ariel* is as proud

as a classic peacock of my old crown; he, or
she, does not attach any value to it, nevertheless, except that of public opinion; Camille is
too thorough a musician to make a mistake on
that point. But with the *Overture de la Tempête*,
Faust, the *Mélodies*, and the *Francs Juges*, it is
quite another thing; there are tears and fire in
them.

My dear Ferrand, if I die, do not turn monk,
as you have threatened you will, I beseech you;
live as prosaically as you can; it is the best mode
of being—prosaic. I saw Germain the other
day, and we talked a great deal about you.
What can I do, what can I say, what can I
write so far away? When shall I be able to
communicate my thoughts to yours? I hear
people singing that wretched *Parisienne*. Some
half-intoxicated National Guards are bellowing
it in all its platitude.

Good-bye; the marble slab on which I am
writing is freezing my arm. I think of unhappy Ophelia; ice, cold, the damp ground,
Polonius dead, Hamlet living. She is very unfortunate! By the failure of the Opéra-
Comique, she has lost more than six thousand
francs. She is still here; I met her recently.
She recognised me with the greatest calm-
ness. I suffered throughout the whole evening

and then I went and told the *graceful Ariel* all
about it.

"Well," said she with a smile; "you were
not upset, were you? You did not faint?"

"No, no, no, my angel, my genius, my art, my
every thought, my heart, my poetic life! I suffered without a groan, for I thought of thee; I
adored thy power : I blessed my cure; I braved,
in my isle of delight, the bitter waves which
broke against it; I saw my vessel shipwrecked,
and casting a glance at my leafy bower, I blessed
the bed of roses whereon I could lie. And
Ariel, Camille, I adore you, I bless you, in a
word I *love you,* more than the weak French
tongue can say; give me an orchestra of a
hundred performers and a chorus of a hundred
and fifty voices, and I will tell you."

Ferrand, my friend, adieu; the sun has set,
I see it no longer, adieu; more ideas, adieu;
far more sentiment, adieu. It is six o'clock, I
need an hour to reach Camille. Adieu.

XXX.

November 19, 1830.

I am writing you a few lines in haste. I have
called upon Denain, I gave him a hundred
francs on account, for which he gave me a receipt, and I left with him a bill for another
hundred, payable on the 15th of January next.

I have been running about all the evening to arrange for a rehearsal of my symphony the day after to-morrow. At two o'clock on the 5th of December, I am to give a concert at the Conservatoire, in which will be performed the overture to the *Francs Juges*, the *Chant Sacré* and the *Chant Guerrier* out of the *Mélodies*, the scene from *Sardanapale* with a hundred performers for the CONFLAGRATION, and lastly, the *Symphonie Fantastique*.

Come, come; it will be awful! Habeneck will conduct the gigantic orchestra. I count upon you.

The overture to *La Tempéte* will be performed for the second time, next week at the Opéra. Oh, my dear, new, fresh, strange, grand, sweet, tender, brilliant—that is what it is. The storm, or *La Tempéte Marine*, has had an extraordinary success. Fétis has devoted two superb articles to me in the *Revue Musicale*.

He said the other day to somebody who remarked that I had the devil in my body,

" If he has the devil in his body, he has a god in his head."

Come, come—the 5th of December—Sunday ; an orchestra of a hundred and ten performers— Conflagration—*Symphonie Fantastique*—Come, come!

XXXI.

DECEMBER 7, 1830.

MY DEAR FRIEND,

This time you absolutely must come. I have had an unheard-of success. The *Symphonie Fantastique* was received with shouts of applause ; the *Marche au Supplice* was encored ; the satanic effect of the *Sabbat* was overwhelming. I have been so pressed to do it that I shall repeat my concert on the 27th of this month, the day following Christmas Day. You will be there, will you not ? I expect you.

Good-bye; I am regularly upset. Spontini has read your poem of the *Francs Juges ;* he told me this evening that he would much like to see you ; he leaves six days hence.

XXXII.

DECEMBER 12, 1830.

MY DEAR FERRAND,

I cannot give my second concert for several reasons. I shall leave Paris at the beginning of January. My marriage is put off till Easter, 1832, on condition that I do not lose my *pension,* and that I go to Italy for a year. My music has compelled the consent of

Camille's mother.   My dear *Symphonie,* to it I shall owe her.

I shall be at Côte towards the 15th of January. I must absolutely see you; arrange so that we may not miss each other.   You will come to Côte; you will go with me as far as Mont Cenis, or at least to Grenoble; will you not, will you not?

Spontini sent me a superb present yesterday; it is the score of his *Olympie,* worth a hundred and twenty francs, and on the title page he has written with his own hand, " My dear Berlioz, when you look on this score, think sometimes of your affectionate Spontini."

I am in a state of intoxication! Camille, ever since she heard my *Sabbat,* calls me nothing but "her dear Lucifer, her handsome Satan."

Good-bye, my dear fellow; write me a long letter immediately, I conjure you.   Your devoted friend for all time.

XXXIII.

CÔTE-SAINT-ANDRÉ, JANUARY 6, 1831.

MY DEAR FRIEND,

I have been staying with my father since Monday last; and I am now on the eve of beginning my fatal journey to Italy. I cannot bear the idea of this harrowing separation; the tender affection of my parents, and the caresses of my sisters can scarcely distract me. I must absolutely see you before my departure. We shall go at the end of next week to spend a few days at Grenoble, and 1 shall return thence to Lyon, and go down the Rhone to Marseilles, where I shall take the steamer for Civita-Vecchia, about six leagues from Rome. Come and see me either here, or at Grenoble, or at Lyon; answer promptly and pointedly on this subject, so that we may not miss each other.

I shall have so much to say to you about yourself and myself. So many storms threaten both of us, that it seems to me to be necessary that we should be near each other to resist them. We understand each other, and that is so rare a thing.

I left Spontini with great regret; he embraced me and made me promise to write to him from Rome. He gave me a letter of introduction to his brother, who is a priest in the Convent of San Sebastian. I will show you what he gave me.

I am so out of spirits to-day that I must stop. You will write to me at once, will you not?

Oh my poor Camille, my guardian angel, my good Ariel, not to see you for eight or ten months! Why cannot I be carried with her by

the north wind to some savage shore, and sleep
my last sleep in her arms? Good-bye; come, I
beseech you.

XXXIV.

GRENOBLE, JANUARY 17, 1831.

MY DEAR FERRAND,

I have been here for the last two days
with my sisters and my mother. We shall leave
for Côte next Saturday, and I rely upon your
arriving on Monday, or Tuesday at the latest.
I need not tell you how charmed my parents
will be to see you; they expect you, not for a
few hours as you have threatened, but for as
long a time as you can give me. I shall leave
for Lyon at the end of the month, but we will
talk over all that. Until Monday, then. I
have endless messages for you from Casimir
Faure.

XXXV.

LYON, THURSDAY, FEBRUARY 9, 1831.

MY DEAR FERRAND,

Instead of this letter you ought to
have received me, my very self in person. I
reached this place yesterday, fully intending to
go to Belley; I even engaged a seat in the
diligence, and paid the full price down. Finally,
after changing my mind I do not know how

many times, I decided upon not going to see you. In spite of the state of torture in which I am; despite the overpowering desire I have to reach Italy so that I may be able to come back again as soon as possible; notwithstanding the weather and the distance, I should have gone to Belley. But a few random words, which I heard yesterday, made me afraid that I should have a cool reception at the hands of your parents, and that your mother, especially, would be anything but charmed to see me; I consequently renounced my project.

I know absolutely nothing about the reason which prevented your coming to Côte, and consequently I cannot discuss it with you. I awaited you in a fever of impatience; everybody regretted your absence exceedingly, and in a word, has not everything happened for the worst?

I start for Marseilles in four hours' time. I shall return, hissing like a red-hot cannon-ball. Meet me at Lyons; I shall only call at Côte.

My address at Rome will be, Hector Berlioz, student of the Académie de Rome, Villa Medici, Rome.

Good-bye; a thousand maledictions on you, myself, and all nature. Suffering is driving me mad.

XXXVI.

FLORENCE, APRIL 12, 1831.

Oh my sublime friend! You are the first Frenchman who has given me any sign that he is alive since my arrival in this garden, peopled by monkeys, which is called *La belle Italie!* I have this moment received your letter; it has been sent on to me from Rome, and has taken seven days, instead of two, to come here. It is all right—curse it! Yes, everything is right, because everything is wrong! What am I to say to you? I left Rome with the full intention of returning to France, letting my *pension* go to the winds, because I had no letters from Camille. An infernal sore throat kept me prisoner here; I wrote to Rome to ask that my letters might be forwarded, and, but for that, yours would have been lost, which would have been a pity. How do I know whether I shall receive any others?

Do not write to me any more because I cannot tell you where to address your letters. I am like a lost balloon, destined to burst in mid-air, or to be engulfed in the sea, or to be brought to a standstill like Noah's ark; if I reach the top of Mount Ararat safe and sound, I will write to you at once.

You may rest assured that I am longing to see you to the full as much as you are to see me; my vacillation and my struggles to overcome my desire cost me a whole day.

I quite appreciate your disgust and anger in regard to what is going on in Europe. Even I, though I do not take the least interest in it, find myself giving way to an oath! Liberty, forsooth—where is it? where was it? where can it be in this half-hearted world? No, my dear fellow, the human race is too grovelling and too stupid for the sweet goddess to bestow upon it one divine ray from her eyes. You talk to me about music—about love! What do you mean? I do not understand you. Are there such things on earth as those we call music and love? I fancy I have heard, as in a dream, these two words of sinister augury. Un-happy mortal that you are to believe in them; as for me, I believe in nothing at all.

I should like to go to Calabria or Sicily, to enlist under the command of some *bravo* chief or other, even as a simple brigand. At all events I should witness magnificent crimes, robbery, assassination, abduction, incendiarism, instead of all these petty wickednesses and dastardly outrages which turn me sick. Yes, this is the world for me—a volcano, rocks, stolen treasure

heaped up in cases, a concert of shouts of
horror to the accompaniment of an orchestra of
pistols and guns, blood and lachryma-christi, a
bed of lava rocked by earthquakes—that would
be life indeed! But there are not even any
brigands near. Oh Napoleon, Napoleon, genius,
power, strength, will! Why did you not crush
in your iron grasp one more handful of this
human vermin? Colossus with feet of brass,
how would your slightest movement overthrow
all their patriotic, philanthropic, philosophic
edifices! Absurd rabble!

And they speak of thought, imagination, dis-
interestedness, even poetry, as if it all existed
but for them!

Such pigmies to talk of Shakespeare, Beethoven, and Weber! But what a fool am I to
concern myself about them. What is the whole
world to me, except three or four individuals in
it? They may extol themselves as much as they
please; it is not for me to pick them up out of
the mire. Besides, it may all be nothing but a
tissue of illusions. There is nothing true except life and death. I met the old sorceress
out at sea. Our ship, after a sublime storm
which lasted for two days, nearly foundered in
the Gulf of Genoa; a squall laid us on our
beam ends. In a moment I was enveloped, legs
and arms, in my cloak so that I might not be

able to swim; everything was giving way, everything was sinking, within and without. I laughed as I saw the white valleys coming to cradle me in my last sleep; the sorceress came on with a grin, thinking to frighten me, and as I was preparing to spit in her face, the vessel righted—she disappeared.

What am I to talk to you about now? Rome? Well, nobody has died; the brave Transteverini merely wanted to swallow us all up, and set fire to the Académie, under the pretext that we had come to an understanding with the revolutionists to drive out the Pope. Nobody even dreamt of it. We pay a great deal of attention to the Pope! He seems too good to be disturbed. Nevertheless, Horace Vernet armed us all, and if the Transteverini had paid us a visit they would have had a warm reception. They did not even attempt to set fire to the old barrack called the Académie! Fools! I might have helped them — who knows?

Anything more? Yes, here at Florence, on my first visit, I saw an opera called *Romeo é Guiletta*, by a little fop called Bellini; I saw it—that is to say, I did what is called *see* it, and the shade of Shakespeare did not come to exterminate such a shrimp. Ah! the dead come not again!

Then a wretch called Paccini had written a thing called *Vestale*. Lecinius was played by a woman. I had just strength enough to quit the theatre after the first act; but I felt myself all over afterwards to see if it was really I—and it was—Oh, Spontini!

When at Rome I wanted to buy a piece by Weber. I went to a music shop, and asked the proprietor for it.

Weber, *che cosa e? Non conosco? Maestro ilatiano, francese, ossia tedesco?*

Tedesco, I replied gravely.

The man searched for a long time, and then said with a self-satisfied air—

Niente de Weber, niente di questa musica, caro signore.

Idiot !

Ma ecco El PIRATA, LA STRANIERA, *I* MONTECCHI, CAPULETI, *dal celeberrimo maestro Signor Vincenzo Bellini; ecco* LA VESTALE, *I* ARABI, *del Maestro Paccini.*

Basta, basta, non avete dunque vergogua; Corpo di Dio?

What was to be done? Sigh? That is childish. Gnash one's teeth? That has become idiotic. Have patience? That is still worse. One must concentrate a dose of poison, letting a portion of it evaporate so that the rest

may have all the more strength, and then shut
it up in one's heart until the end comes.

Nobody writes to me, neither friends nor beloved. I am here alone; I know no one. This
morning I went to the funeral of the young
Napoleon Bonaparte, the son of Louis, who died
at the age of twenty-five, while his other brother
is a fugitive in America with his mother, the
poor Hortense. Not so very long ago she
came from the Antilles, the daughter of Jose-
phine Beauharnais, a light-hearted Creole,
dancing negro dances on deck to amuse the
sailors. She returns thither now, an orphan, a
mother without a son, a wife without a husband, a queen without a kingdom, desolate,
forgotten, abandoned, and with difficulty saving
her younger son from the counter-revolutionary
axe. Young fools who believe that liberty is
going to restore power to them! There was
chanting and an organ; two things puzzled the
colossal instrument—the one who filled the
bellows with air, and the other who made it
pass through the pipes by putting his fingers on
the keys. The latter, inspired no doubt by the
occasion, pulled out the flute stop and played a
series of lively airs, which resembled the chirp-
ing of a lot of sparrows. You ask me for
music; well, I send you some. It is not in the

least like the songs of birds, though I am as
lively as a chaffinch.

From grave to gay, from lively to severe.

Oh, Monsieur Despréaux!

Good-bye, I see you blushing. I shall re-
:main here for a few days, waiting for a letter

which ought to reach me, and then I shall start.

XXXVII.

Nice, May 10 or 11, 1831.

Well, Ferrand, we are moving at last; more rage, more vengeance, more tremor, more gnashing of teeth, in a word more hell!

You have not answered me; no matter, I am writing to you again. You have made me accustomed to write three or four letters to your one. This is the third since the one you addressed to Rome, which I received a month ago at Florence. Nevertheless, I can scarcely understand how it comes to pass that you have not answered me. I so sorely needed a friend's heart, and I almost thought that you would have come in search of me. My sisters write to me every other day. I have recently received as many as five letters at once, but none from you. I am at a loss to understand it. Hear me— if it is from sheer indolence, from laziness or neglect, it is bad, very bad. I gave you my address— Maison Clerici, aux Ponchettes, Nice. If you only knew, when one enters into life again, or, perhaps, falls into it once more, how ardently one longs to find the arms of friendship open! When the heart, torn and wounded, begins to beat again, with what ardour it seeks another heart, noble and strong, which can help it to reconcile itself to existence. I have so often begged you to answer me by return of post! I never doubted your eagerness to add your consolation to that which I received from all sides, and yet it has failed me. Yes, Camille is married to Pleyel. I am now glad of it. From it I have just learnt the danger I have escaped. What baseness, what insensibility, what villainy! It is the immensity, almost the sublimity of wickedness, if sublimity can ally itself with *ignobility* (a new word, and a perfect one, which I have stolen from you).

I shall return to Rome in five or six days; my *pension* is not lost. I will not ask you again to answer me, because it would be useless; but if you wish to write to me, address your letter as you did the last, Académie de France, Villa Medici, Rome. Tell me, also, if you have heard from your bookseller, Denain, to whom I have only paid a hundred francs out of the sum you owe him. How much do I owe you still? Write and let me know.

Good-bye; in spite of your laziness, I am none the less your sincere, devoted, and faithful friend.

P.S.—My *repertoire* has just been increased by
a new overture. Yesterday I finished the one
to Shakespeare's *King Lear*.

XXXVIII.

ROME, JULY 3, 1831.

At last I have news of you. I was right in
thinking that something extraordinary must
have happened. Switzerland is at your front
door, and its glaciers are so seductive; I can
quite understand how continual must be your
admiration of them. I have had a most picturesque trip from Nice to Rome, two days and
a half along the Corniche route, cut in the
rocks, six hundred feet above the sea which
rolls in immediately beneath without a sound
of its murmurs reaching you, by reason of the
immense elevation. Nothing can be more
lovely or more awe-inspiring than this view. I
derived inexpressible comfort from my return
to Florence, where I have spent so many melancholy hours. I was put into the same room,
and there I found my portmanteau, my music,
and my other belongings, which I despaired of
ever seeing again. From Florence to Rome I
travelled with some good monks who spoke
French very well, and were extremely polite.
At San Lorenzo I left the coach two hours be-

fore its departure, leaving behind me my wearing apparel and everything else that might tempt the brigands, who rule the roost here. I journeyed thus during the whole of the day along the lovely lake of Bolzena, and among the mountains of Viterbo, composing the while a work which I have just committed to paper. It is a *mélologue*, the continuation and conclusion of the *Symphonie Fantastique*. For the first time, I have written both words and music. How sorry I am that I cannot show it to you There are six monologues and six musical movements.

1st. A ballad with pianoforte accompaniment.

2nd. A meditation for chorus and orchestra.

3rd. A scene from brigand life for chorus, single voice, and orchestra.

4th. A song of happiness, for a single voice, with orchestral accompaniment at the beginning and end, and in the middle the right hand of a harp accompanying the air.

5th. The last sighs of the harp, for orchestra alone.

6th and last. The overture to the Tempest already performed at the Paris Opéra, as you know.

For the song of happiness I have made use of

a phrase out of the *Mort d'Orphée*, which you have with you, and for the last sighs of the harp, the small orchestral movement concluding the scene which comes directly after the *Bacchanale*. Will you, therefore, kindly send me that page; only the *adugio* which follows the *Bacchanale*, at the point where the violins take up the *sourdines* and give out a series of *tremolandi* accompanying the distant air allotted to the clarionet and a few chords on the harp; I do not recollect it sufficiently well to write it from memory, and I do want it just as it is. As you will perceive by this, I have sacrificed the *Mort d'Orphée;* I have extracted from it all I liked, and I should never be able to contrive to have the *Bacchanale* performed. Consequently, on my return to Paris, I shall destroy my copy, and the one you have will be the sole and only one, if indeed you keep it. It would be better to destroy it as soon as I have sent you a copy of the symphony and the *Mélologue;* but that means spending at least six hundred francs in copying! Never mind, when I get back to Paris, by hook or by crook you shall have it.

It is agreed, therefore, that you are to copy this piece for me in your smallest hand, and I shall await it in the mountains of Subiaco, where I intend staying for a short time; but address it to Rome. I am going to try, by climbing rocks and crossing torrents, to get rid of that leprosy of triviality which covers me from head to foot in our infernal barrack. The atmosphere which I share with my fellow-*manufacturers* of the Académie does not suit my lungs; I am going to breathe a purer air. I am taking with me a bad guitar, a gun, some quires of ruled paper, a few books, and the germ of a grand work which I shall try to hatch in the woods.

I had a grand plan in my head which I wanted to carry out with your assistance; it related to a colossal oratorio, to be produced at a musical *fête* to take place in Paris, either at the Opéra or at the Pantheon, in the courtyard of the Louvre. It was to have been called *Le Dernier Jour du Monde*. I sketched out the plan and wrote a portion of the words at Florence three months ago. It would have required three or four soloists, choruses, an orchestra of sixty performers in front of the theatre, and another of two or three hundred instruments ranged in amphitheatre fashion at the bottom of the stage.

This is the idea. Mankind, arrived at the last degree of corruption, give themselves up to all kinds of infamy, and are governed despotic-

ally by a species of antichrist. A small number of upright men, led by a prophet, appear in
the very midst of the general depravity. The
despot oppresses them, carries off their young
women, insults their faith, and destroys their
holy books amid a scene of orgy. The prophet
appears, reproaching him for his crimes, and
proclaiming the end of the world and the last
judgment. The enraged despot causes him to
be thrown into prison, and giving himself up
once more to impious voluptuousness, is surprised in the middle of a *fête* by the terrible
trumpets of the resurrection; the dead coming
out of their graves, the distracted living uttering
cries of horror, the world in course of destruction,
and the angels thundering in the clouds, compose the end of this musical drama. As you
may well imagine, we should have to make use
of some entirely novel means. In addition to
the two orchestras, there would have to be four
groups of brass instruments placed at the four
cardinal points of the place of execution. The
combinations will be quite new, and a thousand
effects impracticable with ordinary means would
sparkle from out the mass of harmony.

See if you can find time to write this poem,
which would suit you admirably, and in which I
feel sure you would be magnificent. Very few

recitatives—very few solos. Avoid noisy scenes and those which would require brass, as I do not want that to be heard until the end. Opposite effects, such as religious choirs mingled with dance choruses; pastoral, nuptial, and bacchanalian scenes, but out of the beaten track —you understand.

We need not flatter ourselves that we should be able to secure a performance of this work just when we liked, especially in France; but sooner or later the opportunity would present itself. On the other hand, it would be a source of tremendous expense and an extraordinary loss of time. Think well if you would care about writing such a poem with the possibility of its never being heard. And, whatever you do, write to me as soon as you can.

At the end of this month I will send you a hundred francs, and the remainder, little by little, shall follow.

XXXIX.

ACADÉMIE DE FRANCE, ROME,
DECEMBER 8, 1831.

This is the third! My two former letters have remained unanswered. You did not even let me know of your marriage. But no matter;

under such circumstances I cannot do less than
overlook your inconceivable silence. In the
name of heaven let me hear from you. How
are you, and how do you stand with regard to
that infernal mess? I hope you have not
suffered in any way. I wrote to Auguste at
Naples, but have had no answer. I have just
written again to reassure myself on his account,
but I want you none the less to send me news of
him. I am anxiously waiting your reply. To
ensure its safe arrival, do not forget to pay the
postage as far as the frontier.

Your friend always, in spite of all.

XL.

ROME, 9 P.M., JANUARY 8, 1832.

At last I have a letter from you, after a silence
of seven months and a half; yes, seven months!
I have not had a line from you since the 24th
of May, 1831. What have I done to you? Why
did you desert me so? Faithless echo, why did
you leave so many calls unanswered? I com-
plained of you to Carné, Casimir Faure, Auguste,
and Gounet; I asked all our world for news of
my forgetful friend, and only to-day do I learn
that you are still among the living. You have
now yourself experienced, you say, *all* the joy

and ecstasy that the heart of man can contain;
I firmly believe that you have indeed experienced *all* that it can contain, but *no more;*
if that had been the case, its overflowing would
have reached me. What! Not even to let me
know of your marriage? My parents have not
recovered from their astonishment. I quite
believe, since you so assure me, that my letters
have not reached you; but suppose I had not
written to you, could you, in such a case, have
remained silent? I had just written to Germain
to find out what had become of you; *two letters*
to Auguste, one from Naples and the other from
Rome, have remained, like yours, unanswered.
I only asked him for one single and somewhat
insignificant piece of information—whether he
was dead or wounded.

This morning I re-read the only two letters I
have received from you since I arrived in Italy,
and I have not been able to discover in them
anything to justify the horrid, fantastic fears
my imagination had conjured up. I had
pictured to myself some anonymous letter, some
conjugal prohibition, some absurdity, in short,
which had caused you to depart abruptly from
the temple of friendship, without turning your
head even to say farewell to him who had
accompanied you thither.

And now you waste your breath in trying to prove to me things which are quite clear; assuredly, there is neither absolute good nor absolute evil in politics. Equally certain is it that the heroes of to-day are the traitors of to-morrow. I have known for a very long time that two and two make four; I regret the whole of the space you have allotted in your letter to Lyon; it would have been quite enough to have told me that Auguste and Germain were safe and sound. Now that we are once more in the sanctuary, what are the tumultuous shouts from without to us? I cannot understand your fanaticism on that point. You ask what difference there is between the barricades of Lyon and those of Paris? Precisely the difference which separates the greater from the lesser, the head from the feet. Lyon could not make head against Paris, and is therefore wrong to displease Paris. Paris draws France after her, and consequently can go whithersoever it pleases her.

Enough!

Your *Noce des Fées* is charming in its gracefulness, freshness, and brilliancy. I shall keep it until later on, as this is not the moment for composing music on such a theme. Instrumentation is not sufficiently far advanced, and we must wait until I have *immaterialized* it to some extent. Then the world shall hear of the followers of Oberon·; at this moment I could not struggle against Weber with any chance of success.

As you have not received my first letter, in which I unfolded a certain scheme for an oratorio, I send you the same plan for an opera in three acts. Here is the carcase : you must supply the sinews.

LA DERNIER JOUR DU MONDE.

An all-powerful tyrant on earth; the height of civilization and corruption; an impious court; a handful of religious people, owing their preservation and liberty to the contempt of the sovereign. War and victory : combats of slaves in a circus; female slaves resisting the lust of the conqueror; atrocities.

The chief of a petty religious people, a sort of Daniel reproving Belshazzar, upbraiding the despot for his crimes, announces that the prophecies are about to be fulfilled, and that the end of the world is nigh. The tyrant, scarce so much as incensed by the boldness of the prophet, forces him to be present at a fearful orgy in his palace, at the conclusion of which he proclaims ironically that the end of the world will shortly be seen. With the assistance of his women and eunuchs, he represents the valley of Jehoshaphat; a troupe of winged children blow pigmy trumpets, and pretended dead come out of their graves; the tyrant assumes the character of Jesus Christ and is about to judge mankind, *when the earth trembles ;* real and terrible angels sound the awful trumpets; the true Christ approaches, and *the real last judgment commences.*

The piece should not, nor can it be carried further.

Think well over it before undertaking it, and let me know whether the subject suits you. Three acts will suffice, pourtray the unknown to as great an extent as you can, for there is no success in these days without it. Avoid effects of detail, as they are lost at the Opéra, and if you can, treat the absurd rules of rhyme with the contempt they deserve; leave out rhyme altogether when it serves no useful purpose, *which is frequently the case.* All such pedantic ideas ought to be relegated to the cradle of musical art, which would have thought itself injured if rhyme and well-regulated versification had not been maintained.

I shall leave here at the beginning of May, and shall cross the Alps. I hope to be paid the whole of the Government allowance for this year at Milan; if not, I shall evade the regulations, and shall arrange to pay a visit to France in defiance of them, and then to return to Chambéry for my money at the end of the year.

I shall pay you a visit and will let you have what I still owe you; then I shall go and stay with my parents for a short time; then on to my sister at Grenoble (she has married a judge, M. Pal), and finally to Paris. After a couple of concerts for the production of my *mélologue* with the *Symphonie Fantastique,* I shall proceed to Berlin with all my music, and after that—the future.

I am now finishing a long article upon the state of music in Italy for the *Revue Européenne* (the new name of the *Correspondant,* as you know). Carné asked me to write it in a letter announcing his marriage in Brittany. He must be there now, and his nights are brightened by the rays of the honeymoon. Auguste too! Good!

XLI.

ROME, FEBRUARY 17, 1832.

Has my last letter gone astray, too, my dear friend? I answered the one I received from

you a month ago, the day after it reached me.
Seeing that in it I mentioned a great many subjects, I thought you would have replied on the
spot, but nevertheless, I am waiting still, and
you do not write. What a source of vexation
exile is! Every post for the last fortnight has
been a fresh ground of annoyance. If my letter
has gone astray this time, I am at a loss to
know what we are to do to ensure the safety of
our correspondence. I shall start hence on the
1st of May, and shall see you at the beginning
of June. So far so good, but write!

Germain has told me all about Auguste and
his marriage. Well, he is married! Well, it is
well, but not replying to me is very bad. The
devil fly away with him!

I thought I should be able to fill these three
small pages, but I have no other idea than that
of reproaching you for your laziness, and then
my courage fails me. Good-bye, all the same.

XLII.

Rome, March 26, 1832.

I am in receipt of your letter, my dear Humbert, and of the confession of your sublime
laziness. Will you never cure yourself of it?
If you only knew what a dreary punishment
exile is, and how the " sad hours seem long "'

in my stupid barrack, I doubt whether you would make me wait so for your replies.

You have read me a nice homily, but I assure you that you are on the wrong scent, and that you need not be apprehensive of my taking to a calotte, as you seem to imagine I shall. I shall never be an admirer of what is ugly ; of that you may rest assured. My remarks about rhyme were only intended to put you at your ease, for it annoys me to see you employing your time and your talents in a useless and futile conquest over such unprofitable difficulties. You know as well as I do that a thousand instances exist where verses set to music are so arranged that the rhyme, and even the hemistich, completely disappears ; what then is the use of the versification ? Well-balanced and rhyming verses are in their proper place in pieces of music which do not admit, or scarcely admit, of any repetition of the words ; then and then only, is versification apparent and sensible ; under no other circumstances can it be said to exist.

There is a great difference between verses *spoken* and verses *sung.* In regard to the purely literary aspect of rhyme, it is beyond my province to enter into any discussion with you on that subject. I will only say that I firmly believe we owe the existing horror of blank verse to education and habit; do not forget that three-fourths of Shakespeare is in blank verse, that Byron wrote in it, and that the *Messiade* of Klopstock, the epic masterpiece of the German language, is also in blank verse. Quite recently, also, I read a French translation in blank verse of Shakespeare's *Julius Cæsar*, and although, from your remarks about it, I fully expected to be disgusted, it did not shock me in the least. Such is the effect of habit, that the rhyming Latin verses of the Middle Ages are looked upon as barbarous by the very people who are horrified by French verse, which is not in rhyme. But enough on this head.

So you agree to my subject. Well, you have an incredible field of grandeur and wealth open to your imagination. It is all virgin soil, because the scene lies in the future. You may draw upon your imagination as much as you please in respect of manners, habits, state of civilisation, arts, customs, and even costumes, a point by the way, which is not to be despised. You have it in your power, therefore, to seek out the *unknown*—nay, you ought to do so, for there is such a thing as the unknown ; everything has not been discovered. In the matter of music, I am going to clear a Brazilian forest, where I promise myself untold wealth ; we shall advance like bold pioneers as long as our material forces will let us. I shall see you some time in May; shall you have sketched out anything by that time ?

I am going to make another excursion to Albano, Frascate, Castel-Gaudolfo, &c., &c.— lakes, plains, mountains, old sepulchres, chapels, convents, smiling villages, clusters of houses perched on rocks, the sea as my horizon, silence, sunshine, perfumed air, the birth of spring—it is a dream of fairy land !

I took another splendid trip a month ago among the lofty mountains on the frontier; one evening, while sitting by the fireside, I wrote in pencil the little air I now send you. On my return to Rome it was so successful that it is sung everywhere, from the *salons* of the Embassy to the studios of the sculptors. I hope it will please you; this time at all events, you will not find the accompaniment difficult.

Good-bye, my dear friend; I hope to hear from you again before the 1st of May, the date fixed for my departure. To ensure the safe delivery of your letter, address to Florence, *posta firma,* and make due allowance for postal delays.

XLIII.

TURIN, MAY 25, 1832.

MY DEAR HUMBERT,

Here I am, quite close to you, and on Thursday next I shall be at Grenoble. I hope our meeting will not be delayed; for my part, I will leave no stone unturned to hasten it; send me a line on the subject to Côte-Saint-André. I was very much disappointed, but scarcely surprised, at not finding any letters from you at Florence; why are you so incorrigibly idle? I made a point of your not failing to write to me.

No matter—I see the Alps.

Your head has plenty of subjects revolving in it now; does it work much? More than I wish, most assuredly. But after all, why wish for moral uniformity among created beings; why efface individuality? In truth, I am wrong. Let us follow out our destiny—all the more so, seeing that we cannot do otherwise. Have you any news of Gounet? I have not heard from him since the cholera made its appearance. I trust, however, that he has come off scot-free.

And Auguste the silent? If I write to him from this time henceforth, may my two hands wither! I would not have believed him capable of such conduct.

How superb, how rich are the plains of Lombardy! They have awakened in me poignant memories of our halcyon days, "like an idle dream that has fled."

At Milan I heard, for the first time, a vigorous orchestra; there was a beginning of something like music, in execution at least. But the score of my friend Donizetti may go with those of my friend Paccini and my friend Vaccai. The public is worthy of such productions. They talk as loudly during the performance as they do at the Bourse, and their sticks keep up an accompaniment on the floor, almost as loud as that of the big drums. If ever I write for such blockheads, I shall merit my fate; there is nothing more degrading for an artist. What humiliation!

As I came out, the divine lines of Lamartine occurred to me (he is speaking of his poetical muse):

Non, non, je l'ai conduite au fond des solitudes,
Comme un amant jaloux d'une chaste beauté :
J'ai gardé ses beaux pieds des atteintes trop rudes
Dont la terre eût blessé leur tendre nudité.
J'ai couronné son front d'étoiles immortelles,
J'ai perfumé mon cœur pour lui faire un séjour,
Et je n'ai rien laissé s'abriter sous les ailes
Que la prière et que l'amour.

That comprehends all poetry, and is worthy of it.

Good-bye, my dear and excellent friend. To our speedy meeting. Will you give my compliments to your wife. I am very anxious to make her acquaintance.

XLIV.

CÔTE, SATURDAY, JUNE, 1832.
MY DEAR, MY VERY DEAR FRIEND,

I have been here for a week; I have received your letter; I will pay you a visit, but I do not know when; probably in about a week. Do not expect me before Monday in next week; I do not know how I shall go to Belley, possibly on foot, by the Abbrets.

We shall have plenty of talking when I meet, so I will hold my tongue for the present.

XLV.

CÔTE, FRIDAY, JUNE 22, 1832.
MY DEAR FRIEND,

Do not be angry; it is not my fault. As I was getting ready to start, my sister arrived on a visit to my father in honour of me; you can quite understand how impossible it was for me to absent myself from the family gathering. Now, a very violent tooth-ache, which prevented my sleeping during the whole of one night, keeps me confined to my room for I do not know how long; I have a cheek like a bowl.

There is only one thing to be done; write to me on your return to Lyon, and I promise you to start at once if I am able to go out.

Duboys, too, has renewed the invitation he gave me at Rome, to pay him a visit at his country-house at Combe, but that will not come off until after I have seen you.

I have just received a letter from Gounet, about whom I have been rather anxious since the outbreak of the cholera and the riots. He is all right.

XLVI.

GRENOBLE, JULY 13, 1832.

Well, my dear friend, we are not to meet after all! What infernal spell has been cast over us? I have been here for some days past, expecting the news of your return to Lyon, and Madame Faure tells me that you are not there yet! At all events, write to me, I beg of you; send me news of yourself. I am dying of weariness. I went and spent a day in the country with Duboys, when we talked a great deal about you. His wife is passable, but nothing more. Since my return from Italy I have been living in the midst of the most prosaic, withering world! In spite of my entreaties to be allowed to do nothing, they are pleased, they are determined, to talk to me incessantly about music, art, and poetry, terms which these people make use of with the greatest *sang-froid;* you would imagine they were talking of wine, women, riots or other such tomfooleries. My brother-in-law is especially loquacious, and almost kills me. I feel as if I were isolated from all the world by my thoughts, passions, loves, hates, contempt, head, heart, and everything. I am looking for you, I am waiting for you; let us meet. If you are likely to stay at Lyon for a few days, I will join you there; that will be better than going to Belley on foot as I intended; the heat renders such a project almost impossible.

I have so much to say to you, both about the present and the future; we absolutely must come to an understanding as soon as possible. Time and tide wait for no man, and I fear much that you are going to sleep.

I have two hundred and fifty francs to give you; I should have sent them to you long ago if I had known how, and if I had not expected to see you from one day to another. Tell me what I am to do. Casimir Faure has married a charming little brunette from Vienna, whose name was Mademoiselle Delphine Fornier, and who has two hundred and fifty thousand good qualities. He is going to live in Vienna.

I am going to return to Côte shortly, so you had better send your answer there, and do not forget to address me by my two names, so that the letter may not appear to be for my father. Good heavens, how the heat stupifies one !

XLVII.

CÔTE, OCTOBER 10, 1832.

In a word, my dear Humbert, you must come sooner than we agreed. I have reflected that, by not starting for Paris until the middle of November, I shall run the risk of missing my concert; consequently, I shall leave at the end of this month. Come without fail in the last week in October ; we shall have time to put our batteries in position and take a clear aim into the future. After that I will accompany you as far as Lyon, where we shall separate thoroughly saturated with each other. Write to me at once on receipt of this note, and tell me the exact day of your arrival. My parents have too agreeable a recollection of you not to be delighted at the prospect of your visit; they desire me to tell you how impatient they are to see you again. My eldest sister will not be here then, to her great regret, for she appreciates you highly. By way of compensation, I count upon your brother; do not fail to bring him. Bring with you the volumes of *Hamlet, Othello, King Lear,* and the score of *Vestale;* they will all be useful to us.

I dare not hope that you have any portion of your grand dramatic machine ready to show me, notwithstanding your promise. After all it does not matter; only come, and write to me beforehand.

Give my kind regards to your parents, and especially to your charming wife. Remember me to your brother.

XLVIII.

LYON, NOVEMBER 3, 1832.

After all we have not met! I leave this evening for Paris. I have been wandering about in the mud of Lyon since yesterday, and during the whole of the time I have not had a single idea which has not been oppressive and melancholy. Why are we not together to-day? That might, perhaps, have been possible. But I could not let you know the exact day I should pass through this place, as I did not know it myself twenty-four hours beforehand.

Last night I went to the Grand Théâtre, where I was deeply but painfully affected by hearing a worthless orchestra, during a worthless *ballet*, play a fragment of Beethoven's *Pastoral Symphony* (*The Return of Fine Weather*). It seemed to me as if I had discovered in some disreputable haunt the portrait of an angel, and that angel the subject of my dreams of love and enthusiasm. Ah, this comes of being away for two years!

I verily believe I shall go mad when I listen to real music once more. I will send you the *mélologue* as soon as it is printed. You sent me word of some newspapers which I ought to secure, and whose editors are known to you; let me have a line on that subject as soon as possible, addressed to Gounet, No. 34 or 32, Rue Saint-Anne, putting the letter for me under cover.

I am suffering cruelly to-day. I am all alone in this huge town. Auguste lost his wife's young brother the day before yesterday, who died of consumption; he is much affected by it.

Oh, how lonely I am! How I suffer inwardly! What a wretched organization is mine! A regular barometer, now up, now down, subject to the variations of the atmosphere, whether gladsome or dull, of my all-absorbing thoughts.

I feel convinced that you are doing nothing in connection with our great work, and yet my life is ebbing away, and I shall have accomplished nothing great ere it closes. I am going to see Véron, the Director of the Opéra. I shall endeavour to come to terms with him, and draw him away from his mercantile and administrative ideas. Shall I succeed? I do not flatter myself in the least that I shall. My concert will take place in the early part of December.

Adieu, adieu; remember me.

XLIX.

PARIS, MARCH 2, 1833.

Thank you, my dear friend, for your affectionate letter. I did not write to you for the reason which you have divined. I am completely absorbed by the anxieties and annoyances of my position. My father has refused his consent, and has compelled me to make my request in legal form.

Henriette throughout this business is displaying an amount of dignity and force of character beyond reproach. She is persecuted by her family and friends even more than I am by mine in their efforts to withdraw her from me.

When I perceived to what lengths all this was being carried, and witnessed the daily scenes of which I was the cause, I felt inclined to sacrifice myself; I sent word to her that I was capable of renouncing her (which was not true, as it would have killed me) rather than cause any unpleasantness between her parents and herself. So far from accepting my offer, she was grievously vexed about it, and its only result has been to make her fonder of me than ever. Ever since this happened her sister has left us in peace, and when I appear she disappears.

Her affairs have taken a most unfortunate turn ; a performance was arranged for her benefit which might have brought in something ; I had arranged a tolerably attractive concert for her during one of the intervals, and everything was going on well when, at four o'clock yesterday, as she was returning from the office of the Minister of Commerce in a carriage, she attempted to get out before her maid could assist her; her dress caught, her foot slipped on the step, and she broke her leg above the ankle joint.

She suffered dreadfully during the night, and this morning when Dubois came to readjust the splints, she could not restrain her screams ; I think I hear them still. I am almost beside myself. To describe my anguish is an impossibility. To see her in suffering and so unhappy, and yet to be unable to do anything for her, is terrible !

What sort of destiny is awaiting us ? Fate evidently intends us for each other, and I will never leave her so long as I have life. The more unfortunate she is, the more will I cling to her. If to the loss of her fortune and talent that of her beauty were to be added, I feel that I should love her still the same. It is an inexplicable feeling ; though she should be abandoned by heaven and earth, I should still remain as loving, as adoring, as in the days of her glory and her fame. Do not even say a word against this love, my friend, for it is too deep and too full of poetry to be treated by you with aught but respect.

Good-bye; write to me and tell me all about your fresh difficulties; let us only talk now about what touches us most nearly. The whole of the music is not stereotyped yet; I will send it to you as soon as it is finished.

L.

Paris, June 12, 1833.

Thank you again and again, my dear Humbert, for all your anxiety and your answering friendship. Gounet told me a day or two ago that he had received a letter for me from you, but that, by some inconceivable fatality, it had got mislaid in his room, and could not be found anywhere. Your note, which he showed me, made me understand how anxious you have been about me. I am really to blame for not having written to you for so long, but you know how absorbed I am, and how my life varies; one day well, calm, full of poetry and dreams; the next distracted, wearied, a mangy, snarling cur, sick of life and ready to put an end to it if I had not ecstatic happiness in ever-approaching prospect, an eccentric destiny to accomplish, firm friends, music, and, last but not least, curiosity. My life is to me a deeply interesting romance.

You want to know what I do with myself? In the daytime, if I am well, I read or sleep on my sofa (for I am in very good lodgings now), or I scribble a few pages for *L'Europe Litté-raire*, which pays me very well. At six o'clock in the evening I go to Henrietta ; she is still an invalid and in suffering, which drives me wild. I will enter into details about her some other time. I will merely say now that any opinion which you have formed about her is as erroneous as possible. Her life is a romance of an entirely different kind, and her modes of observation, feeling, and thought are

not the least interesting portions of it. Her
conduct, considering the position in which she
has been placed since her infancy, has been
something marvellous, and for a long time I was
sceptical. But enough on that subject.

I am working heartily at the opera you mentioned a year and a half ago in one of your letters
from Rome, and as since then your uncon-
querable idleness has stood in the way of your
doing anything to it, I have applied to Emile
Deschamps and Saint-Felix, who are hard at
work. I hope this will not annoy you, for I have
been very patient. I have just received a message in connection with this very subject. I
will write again shortly.

LI.

PARIS, AUGUST 1, 1833.

MY DEAR, GOOD, AND FAITHFUL FRIEND,

I am replying to your letter at once.
Jules Benedict, a pupil of Weber, I know very
well, but not *Louis*. In all probability he is
still at Naples, where he resides. I never made
him any proposition whatever in connection
with the *Francs Juges;* I never said to him that
you were the author of it; he is absolutely
ignorant of the existence of any piece called
Mélodie Pastorale. I am in Paris, and have no

intention of leaving for Frankfort. Lose no time in unmasking the impudent thief. The overture is stereotyped; I will send you a copy, but it only comprises the separate parts. You will experience no difficulty in putting them together. I am engaged upon the end of the *Bohémiens* scene; I have an idea in regard to our one-act piece. I will have it translated into Italian, dividing it into three acts, and I will try this winter to induce Severini to bring it out. I am going to arrange a grand concert scheme for this winter. If my mind were entirely free, all would go well; I would defy the *cliques* at the Opéra and the Conservatoire, who are more bitter than ever on account of my articles in *L'Europe Littéraire* on the *grand old man* (Chérubini), and especially because, at the first performance of *Ali Baba,* I went so far as to offer *ten francs for an idea* in the first act, twenty in the second, thirty in the third, and forty in the fourth, adding—

"My means do not allow of my bidding higher; I withdraw."

This attack was noised about everywhere, and even came to the ears of Véron and Chérubini, who love me dearly, as you may well imagine.

My life is still in the same painful and unsettled state; I shall see Henrietta to-night,

possibly for the last time ; she is so unhappy
that my heart bleeds for her, and her irresolute
character and timidity prevent her adopting
any definite course of action.   However, it must
come to an end one way or another; I cannot go
on living thus.   Our tale is a sad one, and be-
sprinkled with tears, but I trust there will be
no more than tears.   I have done all that the
most devoted heart could do; if she is not
happier and in a more settled state, the fault is
hers.

Good-bye, my friend. Never doubt my friendship, for in so doing you would be making a
horrible mistake.

Yes, your *Chœur héroïque* was to have been
played at the Tuileries, but it was not reached
on the programme, *the candles having failed*
before its turn came; the performers were
equally in the dark when my piece ought to have
been played, and the concert was brought to a
conclusion with a repetition of the *Marseillaise*
and that wretched *Parisienne*, which could be
played without being seen.

The first rehearsal of that immense orchestra
took place privately in the Cicéri studios in the
Menus-Plaisirs, and the effect of the *Monde
Entiér* was immense, although one half of the
non-musical singers could neither read nor sing;

I was obliged to leave the room for a moment, so deep was the impression it made upon me. I was within an ace of giving way over the chorus out of *Guillaume Tell, Si parmi nous il est des traîtres.* In the open air, the effect disappears; music is evidently not intended in any way for the street.

Good-bye; let me hear the end of that insolent scheme of the spurious Benedict. Do not forget to remember me to your brother and your parents.

LII.

PARIS, AUGUST 30, 1833.

You are right in not despairing about my future! These cowards do not know that, *in spite of everything,* I observe and improve; that I grow even when bending before the violence of the storm; the wind but strips me of my leaves; the unripe fruit I bear clings too firmly to the branches to fall. Your confidence encourages and supports me.

I forget what I said to you in reference to my separation from poor Henrietta, but it has not taken place; she did not wish it. Since then the scenes have become more and more violent; there was the beginning of a marriage, a civil contract which her detestable sister tore up; despair on her part, and reproaches that I loved her no longer; tired of the struggle, I replied to that by taking poison before her eyes. Fearful shrieks from Henrietta —sublime despair —mocking laughter from me—desire to live once more on hearing her frantic avowals of love —emetic—ipecacuanha—results which lasted for ten hours—only two grains of opium remained! I was ill for three days, but got over it. Henrietta, in despair and wishing to repair the evil she had done me, asked me what I wished her to do, and what line of conduct she ought to pursue in order to put an end to our uncertain position. I told her—she began very well, but for the last three days she has relapsed into a vacillating mood, overcome by the instigations of her sister, and the fear caused by our very unsatisfactory pecuniary position. She has nothing and I love her, and she dares not trust herself to me. She wants to wait a few months—months! Damnation! I do not want to wait; I have suffered too much already. Yesterday, I wrote to her to tell her that if she could not let me fetch her to-morrow, Saturday, and take her to the Mairie, I should leave for Berlin next Thursday. She does not believe that I am in earnest, and sent word that she would answer me to-day. There will be more words, entreaties that I will go and see her, protestations that she is ill, &c., &c. But I shall stand my ground, and she will see that, although I have been as weak as water at her feet for so long, I still have strength to get up, to flee from her, and to live for those who love and understand me. I have done everything for her, I can do no more. I sacrifice everything for her, and she dares not run any risk for me. There is too much weakness and too much *reasoning* in this. Consequently, I shall go away.

An unexpected chance has assisted me to bear up against this terrible situation by throwing me into the arms of a poor young girl, eighteen years of age, charming and enthusiastic, who escaped four days ago from the house of a miserable wretch, who bought her when quite a child, and has kept her shut up like a slave for four years. She is almost dead with fright lest she should fall once more into this monster's clutches, and declares that she will drown herself rather than become his property again. I was told about it the day before yesterday. She is bent on leaving France, and the idea came into my head to take her with me. She heard about me, and wanted to see me; I saw her, and contrived to comfort and reassure her

to a certain extent; I proposed to her to come
with me to Berlin, and, through the interven-
tion of Spontini, to place her in some position or
other among the chorus. She agrees to that.
She is pretty, alone in the world, desperate and
confiding. I will protect her, and do my very
best to take a liking to her. If she loves me I
will torture my heart into feeling a remnant of
affection for her. I shall end by imagining I
love her. I have just seen her; she is well
educated, plays the piano tolerably, sings a little,
talks well, and contrives to infuse somewhat of
dignity into her strange position. What an
absurd romance !

My passport is made out; I have only a few
things to attend to, and then I am off. I must
put an end to the present state of things. I
am leaving poor Henrietta very unhappy and
in a deplorable position, but I have no reason to
reproach myself, and I can do no more for her.
Now, this very moment, I would give my life to
be able to spend one month by her side, loved as
I ought to be loved. She will weep and be in
despair, but it will be too late. She will reap
the consequences of her unfortunate character,
which is feeble and incapable alike of deep
sentiment or strong resolution. Then she will
console herself and discover any number of

faults in me. It is always so. As for me, I must be off betimes, without listening to the qualms of my conscience, which is ever telling me that I am too wretched, and that life is an atrocity. I will be deaf. I promise you, my dear friend, that your oracle shall never be made to lie by me.

I send you what you want; the *Chanson de Lutzow* is stereotyped, as arranged by Weber for the piano. You will put words to it. I was not able to send you my manuscript, because I had given it to Gounet. However, there are scarcely any alterations.

Will you send M. Schlesinger, No. 97, Rue Richelieu, a draft for sixteen francs for the joint parcel for yourself and Roland.

Your sincere and faithful friend for life.

Véron has declined the *Dernier Jour du Monde. He dares not accept it.* I am going to send you the overture to the *Francs Juges.* Liszt has just arranged my symphony for the piano. It is an astonishing piece of work. I will write to you from Berlin.

LIII.

Tuesday, September 3, 1833.

Henrietta has come, and I remain. Our banns are published. In a fortnight all will be

finished, if the laws of man will kindly so permit. I only fear their delays. At last ! ! ! It
was time, I assure you.

We have made a subscription for the little
fugitive. Jules Janin is entrusted with the
special duty of seeing her safely away.

LIV.

VINCENNES, OCTOBER 11, 1833.

I am married ! At last ! After a thousand,
thousand difficulties, and terrible opposition
from both sides, I have achieved this masterpiece of love and perseverance. Henrietta has
since our marriage explained the thousand and
one ridiculous calumnies made use of to set her
against me, and which gave rise to her perpetual indecision. One, among others, inspired
her with a horrible dread ; she was assured that
I was subject to attacks of epilepsy. Then
somebody wrote to her from London to say that
I was mad, that all Paris knew it, that she
would be lost if she married me, &c., &c.

In spite of all, we both of us listened to the
voice of our hearts, which spoke out more
firmly and truly than these discordant cries,
and now we are praising each other for having
done so.

There are not many instances of so original a
marriage as ours, and it will upset a number of

sinister forebodings. We shall go together this winter to Berlin, whither my musical affairs summon me, and where an English theatre is to be established, in connection with which certain proposals are to be made to Henrietta.

Will Spontini help us, or, at all events, will he refrain from opposing us? I hope so. Before I leave I shall give some wretched concert or other, and will let you know all about it. Oh, my poor Ophelia, I love her tremendously! I believe that as soon as we have got rid of her sister, who is always more or less troublesome to us, we shall lead a life which may, it is true, be laborious, but will be happy, and right well have we earned it.

Write to me, my friend, at the same address. I am actually at Vincennes, where my wife is taking advantage of the fine weather to recruit her health by means of long walks in the park. I pay a visit to Paris every day; our marriage has made a prodigious sensation there; nothing else is talked about.

Your Unalterable Friend.

LV.

Paris, October 25, 1833.

My friend, my good, my worthy, my noble friend! Thank you, thank you, for your letter, so frank, so touching, so tender. I am pressed, horribly pressed by urgent business, which makes me run all over Paris all day long, but I cannot resist the need I feel to thank you at once for your heartfelt outburst.

Yes, my dear Humbert, I *believed* in spite of you all, and my faith has saved me. Henrietta is a delicious being. She is Ophelia herself; not Juliet, for she has not her passionate ardour; she is tender, and sweet, and timid. Sometimes, when we are alone and silent, she resting on my shoulder, with her hand on my forehead, or in one of those graceful attitudes which no painter ever dreamt of, she weeps amid her smiles.

" What is the matter with you, darling ? "

"Nothing. My heart is so full. I cannot help thinking how dearly you bought me, and how you have suffered for me. Let me weep, or I shall choke."

And I listen to her weeping softly until she says to me, " Sing, Hector, sing."

Then I begin the *Scène du bal,* of which she is so fond.

The *Scène aux Champs* makes her so sad that she does not care about hearing it. She is a sensitive being. Truly, I never imagined that such impressionableness could exist, but she has no musical education, and, would you believe it? she delights in listening to certain of Auber's commonplaces. She does not consider them beautiful, but pretty.

What charmed me most in your letter was your asking me for her portrait; I will certainly send it to you. Mine is being engraved, and as soon as it appears you shall have it. I am alone in Paris to-day; I have just come from Vincennes, where I have left my wife until this evening. I shall be overjoyed in showing her your letter, and I am sure that she will appreciate it, especially the passage about the theatre, her dearest wish having *always* been to quit the stage.

I am going to find out what it will cost to have the *Fantasie dramatique* on the *Tempête* copied. I would rather you had that than mere fragments of the *Symphonie*, because it is a complete work. Besides, Liszt has just arranged the entire *Symphonie* for the piano alone. It is to be stereotyped, and will suffice to refresh your memory.

Good-bye. Write to me often. It will give

me much pleasure to answer you, and tell you about the heaven I dwell in; you alone are wanting there. Oh! if—but that must keep. If there be anything beautiful and sublime on this earth, surely it is love and friendship as we understand them.

The *Francs Juges* is still lying on my table, and I need not tell you how sad it makes me to see your verses, so exquisitely condensed and so musical, lying buried and useless. I have written the *Bohémiens* scene, inserting in it the chorus, *L'ombre descend*, with which the second act opens. It makes a stupendous chorus, and the rhythm is peculiar. I am almost sure it will be effective. I will produce it at my next concert.

I need not see Henrietta to be able to tell you, from her, that she fully appreciates all you have written about her and about me.

Farewell, dearest Horatio. Remember me, I'll not forget thee.

LVI.

WEDNESDAY, MARCH 19, 1834.

Idleness is not responsible for my not having written to you, my friend, since your last letter crossed mine; on the contrary, a superabundance of work has been the cause. The day before yesterday I wrote for thirteen hours without stopping. I am just at the end of the symphony with principal viola part, for which Paganini asked me. I originally intended that it should be in two parts; then a third occurred to me, and subsequently a fourth. I hope, however, that I shall stop there. I have still a good month's continuous work before me. Every day I receive the *Réparateur* from the Vicomte A. de Gouves. You ask me to furnish you with the means of keeping your engagement, but I can send you no other musical news than that which you can find every day in the article in the *Rénovateur*. Write something about the *mise en scène* of *Don Giovanni* at the Opéra, but say, what my position prohibits me from stating, that all the artists without exception, and especially Nourrit, fall lamentably short of their respective parts; Levasseur is too heavy and serious; Mademoiselle Falcon too cold; Madame Damoreau passive and worthless as an actress, and obnoxious by her stupid grace notes; and everybody, except the chorus which is inimitably good, wanting in warmth and movement. The final duet between Don Giovanni and the Commendatore is alone remarkable on the score of execution. The younger Dérivis is very good as the Commendatore. Touch upon the *ballets*, and add that the music of them (composed by the elder Castil Blaze !) is infamous; you cannot give the composer's name as it is almost a secret at present.

Say a word or two about the absurd conduct of the management, which amuses itself by spending its money in the reproduction of works familiar to everybody, and refuses to give us a *new* work capable of interesting the friends of art. The resumption of *La Vestale* by Mademoiselle Falcon is to take place a fortnight hence. It will create a very different effect from *Don Giovanni*, because it is really a great opera, written and instrumented consistently, and, well, because it is *La Vestale*. Allude to that incredible quartet, the four brothers Muller, who play Beethoven after a fashion hitherto unknown.

The *Symphonie*, arranged by Liszt, has not appeared yet. I will send it to you, as well as the *Paysan Breton*, as soon as it is printed. And so you have no idea for a new opera? What, not one?

Good-bye. Yours ever and from the bottom of my heart.

P.S.—I have just written a lengthy biography of Glück for the *Publiciste*, a new paper like the old *Globe*, which is to appear to-morrow. I will send you a copy of it.

LVII.

MONTMARTRE, MAY 15 OR 16, 1834.

I am writing to you at once after reading your letter, my friend, for the purpose of justifying myself. You are angry, and you would have every reason to be so if I really deserved the reproaches you heap upon me.

Shortly after the disturbance at Lyon,* a painter of my acquaintance, who was on his way to Rome, took charge of a letter to Auguste, in which I asked him for news of himself, and consequently of you. I am very disagreeably surprised to find that this letter has never reached its destination. Tell him so if you see him.

As I did not receive any reply from Auguste, I was going to write to you direct, and you have only anticipated me by a few days. I am almost dead with worry and work, compelled by my present circumstances to scribble at so much a column for these rascally papers, which pay me as little as they possibly can; I will send you shortly a life of Glück, with our famous bit of *Telemaco*, which is appended to it.

You want to know what the *Chasse de Lut-zow* is; here it is, as it was sung at the Théâtre-

---

* In allusion to the insurrection of Lyon in the month of April, 1834.

Italien by those beasts of chorus-singers, who destroyed its effect.

Voix seule.

Quels feux loin - tains bril - lent aux pieds des monts? quels cris se mêlent à l'o - ra - ge? L'E - cho plain-tif at - tris - te nos val - lons, qui meurt là - bas? pour qui ces fiers clai - rons son - nent-ils l'heure du car - na - ge? Le noir chas - seur re - pond en ces mots:

The prosody of your lines is not the same in each couplet, and does not go with the music; but rather than alter the musical rhythm it would be better to effect a change in the metre of the poetry. At all events, you can see for yourself which you would prefer. I hope you will never sing the ferocious melody on the scene which your lines describe so well. I am rather afraid of the fate of Walter Scott's Fergus befalling you, and I can see as well as you can what is passing in your heart, far too accessible to certain ideas. If the music publisher of Lyon stereotypes the piece with your words, remember above all things that on no account do I want to appear as if I had corrected or amended Weber, and that he must consequently stereotype the music in exact conformity to the copy I had sent to you by Schlesinger, in which there is no harmony except at the commencement of the chorus.

The whole of the remain ler is for the voice alone. My name must not appear upon it in any form; please be careful about this. The *Hourrah* is not Weber's. You know that, in place of these two bars, there are the two following :—

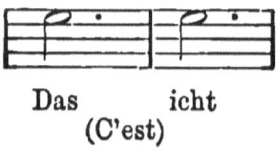

Das   icht
(C'est)

I do not know why I am so wretchedly melancholy to-day, and incapable of answering your letter as I should like. I thank you sincerely for your affectionate inquiries about Henrietta. She is frequently ailing, being in an advanced stage of pregnancy, but, nevertheless, she has been better during the last few days.

My affairs at the Opéra are in the hands of the Bertin family, who have the management of them. The question at issue is the production by me of Shakespeare's *Hamlet* arranged in a superior manner as an opera. We hope that the influence of the *Journal des Débats* will be potent enough to remove the extreme difficulties which Véron may throw in the way. He is now in London; on his return the question will be decided in one way or the other. In the meantime, I have made choice, for a comic opera in two acts, of *Benvenuto Cellini*, whose curious memoirs you doubtless have, and whose character will furnish me with an excellent text from more than one point of view. Do not mention this until it is finally settled.

The *Symphonie* is stereotyped; we are correcting the proofs, but it will not appear before the return of Liszt, who has just gone on a visit to Normandy, where he will remain for four or five weeks. I will send it you immediately, together with the *Paysan Breton*, which I have not forgotten, as you suppose, and which you will receive at the same time. I do not want to have it stereotyped; if it had not been for that, you would have had it by this time. I intend to find a place for it in some opera, so do not let any copy of it go out of your hands.

I have finished the first three parts of my new symphony, with principal viola part; I am going to set to work to finish the fourth. I think it will be good and, above all, curiously picturesque. I intend to dedicate it to one of my friends whom you know, M. Humbert Ferrand, if he will kindly permit me so to do. There is in it a *Marche de pélerins chantant la prière du s oir*, which, I hope, will acquire a reputation for itself in the month of December. I do not know when this enormous work will be stereotyped; in any case, I leave you to obtain the consent of M. Ferrand. Everything shall be stereotyped as soon as my first opera is performed. Good-bye; think of Fergus—if not for your own sake, at all events for the sake of your wife and your friends. Give my kind regards to her and to your parents.

Yours ever from the bottom of my heart.

LVIII.

MONTMARTRE, AUGUST 31, 1834.

I am not in the least forgetful of you, but you do not know how absolutely I am a slave to indispensable work; I should have written to you twenty times if it had not been for these infernal newspaper articles, which I am compelled to write for the paltry pieces they bring me in. I have just seen in the newspaper the sad event which has happened to put your courage to the proof, and I was sitting down to write to you when your letter arrived. I will not offer you the empty consolations which are so weak and useless in such a case, but, if anything could soften the blow that has befallen you, it would be the thought that your father's end was as peaceful and calm as you could possibly have desired. You mention mine; he wrote to me recently in reply to a letter from me in which I informed him of Henrietta's confinement and the birth of my son. His reply was as kind as I anticipated, and he did not keep me waiting for it. Henrietta's confinement was a very painful one, and I experienced a few moments of mortal anxiety. However, everything ended well after forty hours of terrible suffering. She thanks you very sincerely for the mention you make of her in each of your letters; for a long time she has been as conscious as I am that the nature of your friendship is as rare as it is noble. Why are we so far from each other?

I have not received any news of Bloc, or of the *Francs Juges*. Ever since the concerts in the Champs-Elysées and the Jardin Turc have taken possession of this overture, it has become so vulgarized in my eyes that I dare not any longer take an interest in its fate.

I have nothing to do with the *ballet* of the *Tempête*; Adolphe Nourrit arranged the programme, and Schneitzoëffer composed the music.

My symphony called *Harold*, with principal part for viola, was finished two months ago, as I thought I told you. I fancy Paganini will find that the viola is not treated sufficiently after the *concerto* manner; it is a symphony on a new plan, and not a composition written for the purpose of affording a brilliant opportunity for individual talent such as his. Still, my undertaking it is due to him; it is being copied now, and it will be performed next November at the first concert I give at the Conservatoire. I reckon upon giving three consecutively. With that end in view I have just finished several pieces for voice and orchestra which, I hope, will make a goodly show in the programme. The first symphony arranged by Liszt is stereotyped, but it will not be *printed* and published until October; then only shall I be able to send it to you. I am going to have the *Paysan Breton* stereotyped, and you shall have it without delay. I will give M. Schlesinger the order to-morrow to send you my articles in the *Gazette Musicale* upon Glück and *La Vestale.*

Do I know Barbier? So well that he has just had to put up with a somewhat unpleasant disappointment through me. I asked Léon de Wailly, a young poet of great talent, and his intimate friend, to write me an opera in two acts founded on the memoirs of Benvenuto Cellini.

He selected Auguste Barbier to assist him, and the two together wrote the most delicious comic opera possible. We all three went, like so many nincompoops, to M. Crosnier; the opera was read in our presence, and *declined*. We think, notwithstanding the protestations of M. Crosnier to the contrary, that I am the cause of the refusal. I am looked upon at the Opéra-Comique as a *pioneer*, an overthrower of the national style, and they will have none of me. Consequently, the words were declined, so that they might not be placed in a position to accept the music of an idiot.

I have, however, written the first scene, *Le Chant des Ciseleurs de Florence*, with which they are all completely infatuated. It will be heard at my concerts. This morning I read to Léon de Wailly the passage in your letter referring to Barbier, who is now on a tour through Belgium and Germany. Just as he was leaving, Brizeux arrived from Italy, as much in love as ever with his dear Florence. He brings us some new poems; I hope they may be as charming as his *Marie*. Have you read that? Have you read Barbier's last work on Italy,

Divine Juliette au cercueil étendue,

as he calls it? It is entitled *Il Pianto*. It, too, contains some lovely passages. I confess

that I was very much astonished at your not
sharing my enthusiasm over *Les Iambes* when I
recited some extracts to you. It is wonderfully
beautiful. Send me your *Grutli.* I will not fail
to introduce it to him, as well as to Brizeux,
Wailly, Antony Deschamps, and Alfred de
Vigny, whom I see more regularly than the
rest. I seldom meet Hugo ; he is too domineer-
ing. Dumas is a hare-brained creature. He is
on the point of starting with Baron Taylor to
explore the shores of the Mediterranean.
The Minister has placed a vessel at their disposal for this expedition. *L'Adultère* will consequently remain in repose at our theatres for a
year at least. Léon de Wailly is not in the least
disheartened ; he is going, in conjunction with
the younger Castil Blaze, who is not at all like
his father, to complete the plan of a grand opera
in three acts for me ; it will be based on a historical theme, not yet trenched upon, and after
much the same style as the one we asked Véron
to do ; we shall see if a more propitious fate is in
store for it. It must come to something; I am
not uneasy on that score. If I had only enough
to live upon, I would undertake works far above
operas. Music has huge wings which she can
never unfold to their utmost extent within the
walls of a theatre. " Patience and length of
time do more than force or rage."

I could write to you all night long, but as I have to be at my oar in my galley during the day-time, I must needs go to sleep.

Henrietta sends you any number of messages thanking you for your good friendship. In return, remember me to your wife and family. Good-bye; my affection is as surely yours as yours is mine.

LIX.

SUNDAY, NOVEMBER 30, 1834.

MY DEAR AND EXCELLENT FRIEND,

I was almost expecting a letter from you, and I am taking advantage of a leisure half-hour this evening to reply to it. I am tired to death, and I have still a great deal to do. My second concert has taken place, and the reception given to your *Harold* quite came up to my expectations, in spite of the performance being rather unsteady. The *Marche des Pélerins* was encored; it now aspires to become the pendant (religious and calm) to the *Marche au Supplice*. *Harold* will, I hope, reappear in all his strength at my third concert on Sunday next, enhanced by a perfect performance. The orgy of brigands which brings the symphony to a conclusion is rather violent; why cannot I let you hear it? There is much of your poetry in it; I feel sure I owe you more than one idea. Auguste

Barbier thanks you heartily for your poems, and is writing to you on the subject.

The *Symphonie Fantastique* has appeared, but as poor Liszt has spent an exorbitant sum on the publication, we have come to an arrangement with Schlesinger that not a single copy is to be given away, so that I do not suppose I shall have even one for myself. The price is twenty francs; shall I buy you a copy ? 1 should like to be able to send it to you without all this preamble, but you know that for some time to come we shall be in somewhat straitened circumstances. However, to judge from the receipts at my last concert, which were 2,400 francs (double the amount taken at the preceding one), I may hope to get something out of the third. All the copying is now paid for, and a heavy outlay it has been. If you like, I will have a complete copy made for you of the *romance* sung by Mademoiselle Falcon at the last concert. It is the one you know as the *Paysan Breton*, with new words by Auguste Barbier. This trifle forms part of an opera which we once thought would be produced at the Opéra this winter, but the intrigues of Habeneck and Co., and the stupid obstinacy of Véron succeeding a period of vacillation, have postponed it *sine die*.

You hint at the *Gazette*, but M. Laforest, who does the articles, is one of my bitterest enemies ; I am well pleased with his silence. Have you read the articles in the *Temps, Messager*, &c., &c. ?

Henrietta is much obliged to you for having mentioned her and, especially, her little Louis, who is by far the sweetest and prettiest child I ever saw. My wife and I are as united and as happy as possible, in spite of our material annoyances. They only seem to make us love each other more. The other day she was within a very little of being made really ill through her emotion during the performance of the *Scène aux Champs* out of the *Symphonie Fantastique ;* she even cried over it the next morning.

LX.

Paris, January 10, 1835.

You ask me to promise to be frank with you always; I am quite sure I have never been anything else. You think, possibly, that pecuniary reasons led to the delay in your receiving the *Symphonie*. If you do, you are entirely mistaken, because when I wrote to say that the work was not published, I told you the truth. I was not introduced to you yesterday, and I know

full well that I never need give myself any uneasiness on that score. In any case, you will
have Liszt's work to-day, and a copy of the
Jeune Patre Breton, with pianoforte accompaniment, will follow shortly. I am publishing the
latter myself, so I do not want your five-and-
twenty francs.

I should like to be able to send you *Harold*,
which bears your name and is not in your possession. The third performance of this symphony made it a greater success than ever, and
I feel sure you would be delighted with it. I
am going to improve it in certain minor details,
and next year, I hope, it will produce a greater
sensation still.

Your tale about Onslow made me blush, but
with indignation and shame for him; Henrietta
was weak enough to cry about it. As a matter
of fact, Onslow, who only once came to Paris in
February or March to spend six months there,
was never in the capital when my concerts were
going on, and consequently never heard my
Symphonie Fantastique. He cannot have read
it, because I have never lent the manuscript to
anybody, and Lizt's arrangement of it for the
piano has only just appeared. All this is very
disgusting as an evidence of bad faith and pedantic prejudice. I am beginning to have a

thorough contempt both for the opposition and the people who carry it on ; when I say a work is bad, I think it so, and when I think it so, I know that it is so. These gentlemen are guided by motives other than those which influence artists; I prefer my lot to theirs. But let us quit the subject.

You have doubtless seen the last article in the *Temps;* it is by d'Ortigue. I think he has taken a wrong view of the subject, though much of his criticism of details is just. For instance, he asserts that there is not the shadow of a prayer in the *Marche des Pélerins*, and merely notices, in the middle of it, some harmonies overlaid after the manner of Palestrina. They are precisely the prayer, seeing that all religious music is so sung in the churches in Italy. Moreover, that particular passage made an impression, as I anticipated it would, upon everybody, and d'Ortigue stands alone in his opinion. Ah ! if you were only here ! Barbier and Léon de Wailly are almost entrusted with the task of replacing you in one way, for I know no one who sympathises more than they do with my mode of regarding art.

You do not say a single word about your future or your present. Are you not coming to Paris ? Are you writing anything ? When I see d'Ortigue, I will tell him to write you the letter you want. Failing that, I could send you a long article written by M. J. David for the *Revue du Progrès Social;* he has promised to let me see it, and if I am pleased with it, I will send it to you.

If I had time, I should be hard at work already upon another composition I am meditating for next year, but I am compelled to scribble wretched articles which pay very badly. Ah, if the arts received their due meed of appreciation at the hands of our Government, I should, perhaps, be in a different position. However, it comes to the same thing in the end — time will have to be found for everything.

LXI.

APRIL OR MAY, 1835.

MY DEAR HUMBERT,

I received your letter yesterday. I wrote to you about a month ago to introduce a young artist, named Allard, a very distinguished violinist, who was going to Geneva by way of Belley. In all probability, when he found that you were away, he neither called nor left the letter, unless indeed he is still at Lyon.

You have been to Milan ! I do not like that

great city ; but it is the threshold of mighty
Italy, and I cannot tell you how profoundly I
regret, when the weather is fine, my dear old
plain of Rome, and the rugged mountains I
visited so oft. Your letter has recalled it all.
Why do you not pay a short visit to Paris ? I
should be so pleased to introduce you to my
wife, and she is most anxious to know you.

You ask me for details about our home-life.
Here you have them in a few words—our little
Louis has just been weaned and has come satis-
factorily through the ordeal, notwithstanding
the dismal forebodings of his mother. He can
almost walk alone. Henrietta grows more and
more passionately fond of him, but I am the
only member of the household who possesses
all his good graces ; I cannot go out but he
cries for an hour. I work like a negro for four
newspapers which give me my daily bread.
They are the *Rénovateur*, which pays irregularly,
the *Monde Dramatique* and the *Gazette Musicale*,
which pay but little ; and the *Débats*, which
pays well. Added to this, I have to make head
against the horror of my musical position, and
I cannot find time to compose. I have commenced an immense work called, *Fête Musicale
Funèbre à la Mémoire des Hommes Illustres de la
France*. I have already written two parts out

of the seven of which the work will consist. It would have been all finished long ago, if I had only been able to work at it and nothing else for a month, but I cannot get a single day to myself at present, lest I should be in want of the needful in time to come. And yet, only the other day, some idiots amused themselves at the Barrière du Combat by spending fifteen hundred francs to see a bull and a donkey eaten alive by dogs! These are the exquisites of the Café de Paris, and that is the way these *gentlemen* amuse themselves. If you were not the man I know you to be, I should doubt the possibility of making you understand what my volcano says on the subject.

Véron is no longer at the Opéra. The new Director, Duponchel, is not one whit more musical than his predecessor; however, he has given me his word that he will accept an opera in two acts; he insists upon some important alterations in the *libretto*, but when once they are passed, we shall come to business; in other words, he will have to sign a contract providing for a heavy forfeit, because I have just as much, and no more faith in the word of a director as I should have in that of a Greek or a Bedouin. I will let you know when the matter is settled.

My father and my sister, Adèle, wrote to me a short time ago very affectionately. I do not know what concert you allude to; I have given seven this year. I shall begin again in November, but I shall not have anything new to produce; my *Fête Musicale* will not be finished, and besides, it is written for seven hundred performers. I think both the place and the subject will suit you. I shall give our *Harold* once more. The musical judgment of the Italians astonishes you? They are almost as stupid as the French. In Paris we are now witnessing the triumph of Mussard, who on the strength of his success, and the assurance given him by his public-house associates, thinks himself equal to Mozart. I can quite believe it! Did Mozart ever write a quadrille like the *Brise du Matin,* or the *Coup de Pistolet,* or the *Chaise Cassée?* Mozart died in poverty, which, of course, was only right and proper; Mussard is making at the present time at least twenty thousand francs a year, which is still more right and proper! Lastly, Ballanche—the immortal author of *Orphée* and *Antigone,* two sublime poems in prose, as grand and simple and beautiful as if they were the work of the ancients—poor Ballanche has only just escaped being arrested for a bill of two hundred francs which he could not pay! Think of that, Ferrand. In sober earnest, is it not enough to drive one mad? If I were a youth and my actions only affected myself, I know very well what I should do. But let that pass. Good-bye ; love me always as I love you. Write to me as often as you can ; in spite of my perpetual bondage, I will find time to answer you. My wife, who grows dearer and dearer to me, thanks you for your message ; do not forget to remember me to yours. Oblige me by reading *Chatterton*, by Alfred de Vigny.

LXII.

MONTMARTRE, OCTOBER 2, 1835.

MY DEAR FERRAND,

I am making use of a leisure moment to ask you to forgive me for having been so long silent. I imagine you are angry : at all events, your literary parcel *without any letter* seems to point that way. Or did you mean to retaliate upon me for having sent you the score of the *Francs Juges* without writing to you at the same time? I fear so. Nevertheless, the simple truth is that, what with my cursed newspaper articles, my hundred times cursed rehearsals of *Notre-Dame de Paris*, and the composition of my opera, I have not even time to smoke a cigar. And now you know why I have not written to you. Whatever idea you may have of my shortcomings, I trust you will not appear to think them serious.

I have read with great pleasure everything that you sent me; your lines on the *Grutli*, especially, delighted me more than I can tell you, and between ourselves, Barbier ought to be very proud of the dedication. He is shortly going to publish a new edition of his works, comprising his *Iambes*, *Pianto*, and his new and unknown poems on England. I think you will like them.

There are also some charming things by him in our opera. I am almost at the end of my score, having only one portion, a long one though, of the instrumentation to write. I am now in possession of a *written* promise from the Director of the Opéra that I shall be performed sooner or later; it is merely a question of having patience until after the performance of works which stand before mine; unfortunately, there are three of them. The Director, Duponchel, is more and more infatuated about the piece, but grows more and more distrustful of my music (which he does not know, of course) every day; he trembles with fear. It is to be hoped that I shall upset his calculations, and that the success of my collaborators will enable his self-esteem to recover from the blow. The *libretto* is undoubtedly charming. Alfred de Vigny, the patron of the association, came and spent the day with me yesterday. He brought the manuscript with him in order to go through the poem attentively once more. He possesses rare intelligence and a superior mind, which I admire and love with my whole soul. He will shortly publish the continuation of *Stello ;* do not you admire the style of his last work, *Servitude et Grandeur Militaires ?* How true it is, and how well expressed !

My boy is growing and improving day by day ; my wife is mad about him. Forgive me for having said that; I feel that I have done wrong.

The Coste library has commenced the publication of *Hommes Illustres de l'Italie.* We came to an arrangement that he should write to you to help in it; I do not know if he has done so. I have not seen him for a long time. I will mention it to him one of these days. Your being away is a great mistake. The parts which have already appeared contain, among other remarkable lives, that of Benvenuto Cellini. Read it, if you have not read the autobiographical memoirs of that bandit of genius.

Give my kind regards to Madame Ferrand

and your mother. I hear that you are speculating, or at all events, that you take a certain interest in the industrial speculations in your neighbourhood. So much the better, if you succeed. Write soon; I have been longing to hear from you for a fearful time.

Your sincere and unchangeable friend, whatever you may think.

LXIII.

MONTMARTRE, DECEMBER 16, 1835.

MY DEAR FERRAND,

I am not to blame for having kept you waiting so long for a letter; you can have no idea of what I have to do day after day, and how very little leisure I have, even when I have any. But it is useless to expatiate on that subject; I am sure you do not doubt the pleasure I experience in writing to you.

I met A. Coste, the publisher of *Italie Pittoresque,* yesterday; he told me that it is too late to send in any article for that work, as it is approaching a conclusion, but that if you like to send him any biographies of illustrious men and women for his publication, *Galerie des Hommes Illustres de l'Italie,* which is to come out as a continuation of *Italie Pittoresque,* he will be delighted. Send him the names of the subjects you chose, so as to avoid any chance of their being done twice over, or given to somebody else. As nobody has paid any attention to the women, Coste would be glad if you would devote yourself specially to them. Your articles will be paid for at the rate of from a hundred to a hundred and twenty-five francs; I will do my best to get the hundred and twenty-five for you.

Thank you for your verses; if I can find time, I will try to hit upon a tune to match them.

I should very much like to send you the score of *Harold*, which is dedicated to you. It has been twice as successful this year as last, and it decidedly surpasses the *Symphonie Fantastique*. I am glad I offered you the dedication before I made you acquainted with the work; to introduce it to you will be a fresh delight. Frankly, I have written nothing which will suit you better.

An opera of mine has been accepted at the Opéra; Duponchel is in a good humour; the *libretto* which, this time, will be a poem, is by Alfred de Vigny* and Auguste Barbier. It is deliciously vivacious, and full of colour. I cannot set to work upon the music yet; metal fails

*The name of Léon de Wailly is published as the collaborator of Auguste Barbier.

me as it did my hero (you know, perhaps, that
he is Benvenuto Cellini). In a day or two I
will try to find time to send you a few notes for
the article you want to write, and especially
about *Harold*. I am most successful in Germany, thanks to the pianoforte arrangement of
my *Symphonie Fantastique* by Liszt. I have received a bundle of newspapers from Leipsic and
Berlin, in which Fétis shines brilliantly with
light reflected from me. Liszt is not here.
Besides, we are so intimately connected that
his name would do the article more harm than
good.

Thank you for all you say about my wife and
my son ; I love them more and more every day.
Henrietta is deeply sensible of all the interest
you take in her, but your allusions to our little
Louis delight her most.

P.S.—The two extracts from *Harold* cannot
be taken apart from the remainder without
making nonsense of them. It would be just like
sending you the second act of an opera.

LXIV.

JANUARY 23, 1836.
MY DEAR HUMBERT,

I am so horribly busy that you must
excuse my sending you only a few lines. Thank

you a thousand times for the fresh proof of your friendship; you are just as I have ever known you, an excellent fellow with a very generous heart. After all, everything in this world depends upon chance.

That amiable little M. Thiers has just made me lose the appointment of Director of the Gymnase Musical, which would have brought me in twelve thousand francs a year, and all because he would not allow oratorios, choruses, and *cantatas* to be performed there, on the ground that it would injure the Opéra-Comique.

You ask me what my *Napoleon* is. It consists of some indifferent lines by Béranger which I seized upon because the sentiment of the *quasi*-poetry seemed to me to be musical. I think the music would please you, in spite of the words ; it is extremely grand and melancholy, the end especially so :

Autour de moi pleurent ses ennemis—
Loin de ce roc nous fuyons en silence.
L'astre du jour abandonne les cieux.
Pauvre soldat, je reverrai la France,
La main d'un fils me fermera les yeux.

I wish I could find time to set your energetic lines to music; something striking is needed; unfortunately, I have not a single moment to devote to composition.

LXV.

APRIL 15, 1836.

It is quite true, my dear Humbert, that I have owed you an answer for a long time, but it is also quite true, in the strictest acceptation of the word, that I have not had a moment at my disposal to devote to you. Even now I feel that I shall not be able to tell you one half of all I feel. I am in the same position as regards my sister, to whom I have not been able to write a line for three months.

I am compelled to work tremendously hard for all the papers which pay me for my articles. You know that I now write the musical reviews (of concerts only) for the *Débats;* they are signed H. ***. It is a matter of great importance to me, and the effect they produce in the musical world is really singular; each one is regarded as an event by the artists in Paris. I declined the invitation of M. Bertin to give an account of *I Puritani,* and that wretched *Juive;* I should have abused them too heartily, and have laid myself open to a charge of jealousy. I still keep to the *Rénovateur,* in which I but partially restrain my hatred of all these pretti-nesses. Then there is *Italie Pittoresque,* which has managed to get a contribution from me.

Again, the *Gazette Musicale* worries me every
Sunday for a column of concerts or an account
of some wretched inanity recently published. In
addition to this, I have made innumerable
attempts during the last two months to give a
concert; I have tried every room in Paris,
seeing that the doors of the Conservatoire are
closed against me, thanks to the monopoly
granted to the members of the Société des
Concerts. I know beyond a doubt that it
possesses the only room in Paris where I could
be heard to advantage. I think I shall give a
final evening on the 3rd of May, as the Conservatoire will have finished its concerts by that
date. I have just composed the music for your
scene in the *Francs Juges—Noble amitié.* I
have written it so that it can be sung by
tenor or soprano ; however it may suit a man's
voice, I had Mademoiselle Falcon in my eye
when I wrote it. She will get plenty of effect
out of it ; I will take it to her one of these days.

Forgive me for not having yet sent you the
copies of the *Pâtre Breton ;* I am going to post
them at once. The fact is, I have forgotten
them day after day. This summer I am going
to write a third symphony on an entirely new
and vast plan ; I hope I shall be able to work at
it in freedom.

Your *Harold* is still in high favour. Liszt introduced a fragment of it into his concert at the Hôtel de Ville, and it obtained the honours of the evening. I am very sorry you have not a copy of this score, which is dedicated to you.

I have not sent you the article by J. David because I have not been able to get hold of it. It appeared in the *Revue du Progrès Social*. I really have not time to write what you want in connection with a biographical notice. Besides, the musical papers of Leipsic and Berlin are, apparently, full of my biographies; several Germans who are here have mentioned them to me. They are translations, more or less enlarged, of the one by d'Ortigue.

Talking of d'Ortigue, he is married as you doubtless know. Your wife is very good to appreciate my little song; thank her from me for having given such a kindly reception to the *Petit Paysan*. Henrietta and our little Louis are very well; a thousand thanks for your kind messages.

We often talk of you to Barbier. He is just the sort of man with whom you would like to associate. Nobody could possibly understand more thoroughly than he does the serious and noble side of an artist's mission.

I have had an application from Vienna for a

copy of the score of the *Symphonie Fantastique,*
at any price I like to name; I have replied to
the effect that, as sooner or later I must pay a
visit to Germany, I cannot send it on any
condition.

All the poets of Paris, from Scribe to Hugo,
have *offered* me poems for an opera; the stupid,
vulgar managers alone stand in my way. But
I have patience; one of these days I shall have
my foot on their necks, and then—we shall
see.

You do not say a word about what you are
doing. Are you pleading? Are you travelling?
Have you been to Geneva? To Switzerland?
And what has become of your brother? He is
a second edition of you; I never saw two men
so thoroughly alike as you are.

Have you read *Orphée* and *Antigone* by
Ballanche? Do you know that his imitation of
the antique is of unparalleled beauty and
magnificence? I have been taken up with it
for some months past.

I must leave you now, to betake myself to the
Débats with an article upon Beethoven's symphony in C minor, in which the phrase you
mention occurs. Meyerbeer is expected shortly
to begin the rehearsals of his great work, *Saint
Barthélemy.* I am very anxious to make its

acquaintance. Meyerbeer is the only successful musician who has given any sign of real interest in me. Onslow, who was present at Liszt's concert a short time ago, overwhelmed me with inflated compliments upon the *Marche des Pélerins*. I like to think that he did not mean a word of them. I prefer the open hostility of that kind of man.

Liszt has written an admirable *fantasia* for full orchestra upon the *Ballade du Pêcheur* and the song of the brigands.

LXVI.

APRIL 11, 1837.

May the devil fly away with me, my dear friend, if ever since your last letter I have not sought in vain for ten minutes wherein to write as many lines! You have no idea what this life of hard labour is like. At last I am free for a moment.

You are always the same, my excellent friend, and I thank you for being so; write to me as often as you can, and do not abuse me, but, on the contrary, pity me for having less liberty than you have. Your long and precious letter charmed me; it contained a mass of details which, I assure you, gave me great pleasure.

I will reply to your question about *Esmeralda*

first of all. I have had nothing to do with the composition by Mademoiselle Bertin, absolutely nothing except giving advice and hints as to musical form; nevertheless, the public will have it that I am the author of Quasimodo's air. The judgments of the crowd are fearfully rash.

My opera is finished. It is now waiting until MM. Halévy and Auber shall each of them be kind enough to write an opera in five acts, the production of which, in accordance with my engagement, must precede mine. In the meantime, I am at work upon a *Requiem* for the funereal anniversary of the victims of Fieschi. The Minister of Interior commissioned me to write it. For this immense work he offered me *four thousand francs.* I accepted without making any remark beyond that I should require five hundred performers. After a certain amount of alarm on the part of the Minister, the contract was drawn up, my army of musicians, however, being reduced by fifty. I shall consequently have four hundred and fifty at least. I am finishing the *Prose des Morts* to-day, beginning with the *Dies Iræ* and ending with the *Lacrymosa ;* it is sublimely gigantic poetry. I was intoxicated with it at first, but afterwards I managed to get it under; I have mastered my subject, and I now think that my score will be passably grand. You understand what that ambiguous word demands in justification for its use, but, nevertheless, if you will come and hear me in July I am bold enough to believe that you will pardon my having employed it.

I have had an application from Germany to purchase my symphonies, but I have refused to allow them to be stereotyped at any price before I produce them there in person.

The overture to the *Francs Juges* has just been performed at Leipsic with enormous success; similar good fortune has befallen it in France, at Lille, Douai, and Dijon; on the other hand, the orchestras in London and Marseilles have failed, after several rehearsals, to master it, and have given it up. My two concerts this year have been magnificent, and the success of our *Harold* has been really extraordinary. And now I have given you all my news. I have on my hands articles for the *Débats*, a review in the *Chronique de Paris*, and criticisms in the *Gazette Musicale*, which I have been editing for some weeks past, in the absence of Schlesinger, who is in Berlin. I have no lack of work, you see. I have given up answering letters.

Your poems and your prose novel have interested me greatly; there are some magnificent
passages in them. Gounet comes to see us frequently. He has had a great loss recently; his
young brother, twenty-one years of age, has
died at the school of Saint-Cyr after terrible
sufferings, from the consequences of a dislocated
thigh. Send him a few lines of condolence, if
you can.

I have, also, lost my grandfather, who passed
away quietly at the ripe old age of eighty-nine,
in the presence of my mother and sister. My
uncle is here; he has just been appointed to
the colonelcy of the 11th Regiment of Dragoons.
We see him frequently. What a series of sad
events, mingled with a few subjects for joy or
hope!

Barbier is quite right in comparing Paris to
an infernal tub, in which everything is in a constant state of fermentation and bubble. *A propos,*
his new poem *Lazare,* has just appeared in the
Revue des Deux Mondes. Have you read it?
There are some notable passages in it, quite
worthy of his *Iambes.* He thanks you from
the bottom of his heart for your dedication.

Good-bye, my dear, good friend; write to me,

I repeat, as often as possible, and always believe in my unchangeable friendship.

LXVII.

DECEMBER 17, 1837.

MY DEAR FERRAND,

Flayol wrote to you eight or ten days ago. For that reason I waited patiently, and but for that my letter would have reached you very much sooner. That is a fact. The *Requiem* was admirably played; its effect upon the majority of the audience was terrible; the minority, who neither felt nor understood it, do not quite know what to say; the newspapers as a rule, except *Le Constitutionnel*, *Le National*, and *La France*, on which I have determined enemies, have been most favourable. You were missing and missed, my dear Ferrand, and you would have been well pleased, I think; it is precisely your idea of sacred music. It is a success which popularises me, and that is the great point. It produced a tremendous impression upon people of diametrically opposite feelings and constitutions. The *curé* of the Invalides shed tears at the altar for a quarter of an hour after the ceremony; he wept as he embraced me in the vestry. When it came to the *Jugement dernier*, the startling effect produced by the five orchestras and the eight pairs of kettle-drums accompanying the *Tuba mirum* was beyond description; one of the choristers had a nervous seizure. In truth, its grandeur was terrible. You have read the letter of the Minister of War; I have received I do not know how many others, couched in much the same terms as those I receive from you occasionally, *minus* the friendship and the poetry. Among others, I have one from Rubini, one from the Marquis de Custine, one from Legouvé, one from Madame Victor Hugo, and one, a stupid one, from d'Ortigue, besides very many others from various artists, painters, musicians, sculptors, architects, and prose-writers. Ah! Ferrand, it would have been a happy day if I had had you by my side during the performance. The Duc d'Orleans, according to what his aides-de-camp say, was also very deeply moved. The Minister of Interior has some idea of purchasing my work, which would thus become national property. M. de Montalivet, so I heard to-day at his office, is not disposed to give me the bare four thousand francs, but intends adding a considerable sum to it. How much will he give me for the copyright of the score? We shall soon see.

My turn at the Opéra will, possibly, come soon. This success has had a beneficial effect on my affairs; the principals and chorus-singers are even more decidedly on my side than the orchestra. Habeneck himself is completely converted. As soon as the score is stereo-typed, you shall have it. I think I shall be able to secure a repetition of the greater part of the movements in it at a sacred concert, to be given at the Opéra. It will require four hundred performers, which means an outlay of ten thousand francs, but the receipts are safe.

Let me know, as soon as you can, what you are doing, where you are, and what is becoming of you (if you are not too angry with me for my long silence), how your wife and family are, if you intend coming to Paris, &c., &c.

Your very Devoted and Sincere Friend.

LXVIII.

Paris, September 20, 1838.
My Dear Humbert,

Thank you for writing to me. I am so glad to know that you are still the same, and to think that your friendship is ever watchful from afar, despite the rarity of your letters and your many occupations!

Yes, we were wrong in supposing that the *libretto* of an opera, based on artistic interest and the passion of an artist, could please a Parisian audience. This mistake has had a disastrous result; but the music, in spite of all the clamour skilfully concerted by my secret enemies, has stood its ground. The second and third performances were everything that could be desired. What the article-mongers call my system is no other than that of Weber, Glück, and Beethoven; I leave you to judge what ground there is for so much abuse; they only attack it in this way because I published some articles on *rhythm* in the *Débats,* and because they are delighted to write, on this subject, pages of theory containing as many absurdities as notes. The newspapers *pro* are the *Presse, L'Artiste, La France Musicale,* the *Gazette Musicale,* the *Quotidienne,* and the *Débats.*

My two *prime donne* were twenty times as successful as Duprez, who lost his head so completely that he was on the point of throwing up his part at the third performance. Alexis

Dupont is going to replace him, but he will require nearly ten days to learn the music thoroughly, which causes a somewhat disagreeable interruption in my performances. The result is a re-arrangement of the *repertoire* of the Opéra by means of which I shall be performed very much more frequently with Dupont than I could have been with Duprez. That is a point of the greatest importance; all I want is to be heard very frequently. My music can fight its own battle. You will hear it, I fancy, in December, and you will be able to judge if I am right in telling you now that *it is good*. The overture will bear comparison, I think, with those to the *Francs Juges* and *Roi Lear*. It has always been warmly applauded. It is the question of *Der Freyschütz* at the Odéon over again; I cannot give you a more accurate comparison, although, musically speaking, it may be an ambitious one. It is, however, *less eccentric* and has *greater scope* than Weber.

I wrote an overture to *Rob Roy*, but after I heard it I did not think well of it, so I burnt it. I likewise wrote a mass which appeared to me quite as bad; I burnt that also. There were three or four movements in our opera of the *Francs Juges* which I destroyed for the same reason. But when I say to you, " This or that score possesses all the qualities which give life to works of art," you may believe me, and I am sure you do believe me. The score of *Benvenuto* comes under this head.

LXIX.

SEPTEMBER, 1838.

Ah! Ah! Joy at last! You are really here!

I send you the only ticket I have. Come this evening after the opera to Box No. 35, third tier. It is my wife's box. I will join you there as soon as possible, either during or before the *ballet*. Massol is ill, and is compelled to omit his air.

LXX.

AUGUST 22, 1839.

MY DEAR HUMBERT,

Many thanks for your long and charming letter! The sight of your handwriting on an envelope is always an occasion of rejoicing to me, but this time the rejoicing was all the more joyful because I had waited for it so long. I was at a loss to know what had become of you. Were you in Sardinia, at Turin, or at Belley? I can quite understand the pleasure you must derive from your immense farm, and I, too, often say to myself, *O rus, quando te aspiciam!* But there is nothing more impossible than such a trip just now. It is too far out of my way; I must cross the Rhine instead of the Mediterranean.

Forgive me for writing somewhat hurriedly to you. For the last week I have been seeking an opportunity to chat with you at my leisure, and I am obliged to give up the idea. But I send you a few lines on the subjects in which you are good enough to take an interest.

I have finished my grand choral symphony; it is equivalent to an opera in two acts, and will take up the entire concert; there are fourteen movements in it.

You ought to have received three scores; the *Requiem,* and the overtures to *Waverley* and *Benvenuto.* I have just finished copying the scene of the workmen, *Bienheureux les matelots!* and the minor duet between Ascanio and Benvenuto, for your brother, whom I thank for his kind message. As the score is very simple, and the accompaniment is confined to the strings, it was easy for me to reduce it, and you will have it all alike, but it will cost you a ridiculous sum in postage!

Here is the passage of the oath of the sculptors.

Ruolz has just produced his opera, *La Vendetta,* which Duprez sustained with absolute frenzy, but its success was essentially negative. The entire audience was conscious of the worthlessness of such a composition, but it was allowed to pass without a word. I was hard pushed to write an account of it, but M. Bertin would stand no nonsense, so I was obliged to tell almost the truth. I have not seen Ruolz since.

Talking of articles, read the *Débats* of to-day, Sunday. You will find at the end a homily intended for Duprez, under the name of *M. Débutant*. It will make you laugh.

The ode to Paganini appeared a week ago in the *Gazette Musicale*, but with an atrocious printer's error, which made one strophe unintelligible.

Thank your brother a thousand times for the trouble he has taken in translating Romani. It is marvellously beautiful, and my wife and I have discovered a singular likeness between the colouring of this poetry and that of Moore's Melodies. Tell M. Romani, when you see him, that I admire it heartily.

Spontini is becoming more and more absurd, and foolishly jealous. He wrote an inconceivably ridiculous letter to Emile Deschamps the day before yesterday. He has left for Berlin, after having disenchanted his most ardent admirers here. Where the devil has genius put itself? It is true that she has been homeless for a long time. But, after all, *La Vestale* and *Cortez* are still to the fore.

Good-bye, my dear friend, I will keep you posted up about the rehearsals of *Roméo et Juliette*. I am occupied now in correcting the copies, and I am going immediately to call upon a German writer, who has undertaken the translation of my *libretto*. Emile Deschamps has written me some very fine verses, with an occasional exception. I will send them to you.

LXXI.

LONDON, FRIDAY, JANUARY 31, 1840.

MY DEAR HUMBERT,

I have a little leisure to-day, and am less tormented by the wind than I have been for the past ten days, consequently I am going to reply to you in as cheerful a vein as I can. Your congratulations, so full of warmth and real friendship, failed me, and I missed them incessantly. I am content; my success is complete. *Roméo et Juliette* has drawn tears once more; there was a vast amount of weeping, I assure you. To go into detail about the three concerts would take up too much time and space; suffice it to say that the new work roused an inordinate amount of passionate controversy, and effected some notable conversions. I need not add that the nucleus of my inveterate enemies remained as obdurate as ever. An

Englishman gave one of Schlesinger's servants
thirty francs for the little deal *bâton* I used
when conducting the orchestra. In addition to
this, the London press has behaved splendidly
to me.

For the three evenings I had to pay the performers twelve thousand one hundred francs ;
the receipts amounted to thirteen thousand two
hundred, so out of this latter sum I only got
eleven hundred francs. Is it not a melancholy
thing that so splendid a result, taking into consideration the limited size of the room and the
manners and customs of the public, should turn
out to be so paltry when one looks to it for
means of subsistence ? Serious art is decidedly
incapable of maintaining its disciples, and it will
continue to be so until a Government arises
which can appreciate how unjust and horrible
such a state of things really is.

I send you the *libretto* by Emile Deschamps
and the couplets of the prologue, the only fragment I care about publishing ; you can sing it to
yourself. You will find the accompaniment very
easy. Paganini is at Nice. He wrote to me a
few days ago ; he is enchanted with his *work*.
It really is *his*, for it owes its existence to
him.

Alizard has had a positive triumph in his *rôle*

of the good monk, Friar Laurence, a name
which has stuck to him. He not only displayed
a marvellous comprehension of the beauties of
this Shakespearian character, but he succeeded
in conveying them to others. His chorus was
superb at times, but the spirit, precision,
delicacy, brilliancy, majesty, and passion displayed by the orchestra simply astounded the
audience. I will send you shortly the overture
to *Roi Lear*, the full score of which will shortly
be published.

I was asked by the Opéra to write the music
for a *libretto* in three acts by Scribe. I took the
manuscript, but I afterwards changed my mind,
and sent it back ten minutes afterwards without
reading it. It would take up too much time to
tell you my reasons. The Opéra is a school of
diplomacy. I am improving. But, joking
apart, my dear Ferrand, this sort of thing
wearies, disgusts, shocks me, and makes me in-
dignant. Fortunately, we shall very possibly
have a change soon; the management is ruin-
ing itself. Aguado does not want to have anything more to do with his two theatres, but he
does not know how to get them off his hands.
The Italians are driven to bay. In the meantime you live in your island; you see the sun,
the orange-groves, and the sea. Come to Paris

for a while. If you only knew how melancholy I am in it. I suppose I shall get over it.

Thank your brother for his kind message. Try to bring him with you. Give my kind regards to Madame Ferrand. Henrietta is rather anxious; Louis is not well, and the doctor cannot make out what is the matter with him. I hope to see him all right again soon.

On Thursday next the *Gazette Musicale* is going to give its subscribers a grand orchestral concert. I am to conduct. Your *Symphonie d'Harold* and the overture to *Benvenuto* will find a place in the programme.

I am so dreadfully melancholy that nothing makes the slightest difference to me; what is going to happen to me? Most probably nothing. Well, we shall hear all about everything some day or other. Come what may, I love you sincerely; never doubt that.

P.S.—I see Gounet very seldom, and he is generally very melancholy. He is becoming really old, more so than you would believe. Barbier has just published another volume of satires, but I have not yet read it. We were both of us *dancing* at Alfred de Vigny's the other night. How wearisome it all is! It seems to me that I must be a hundred and ten years old.

LXXII.

OCTOBER 3, 1841.

MY DEAR HUMBERT,

Will you believe me when I tell you that since the moment I received your letter, which gave me such genuine pleasure, I have not been able to snatch a single hour to devote to you? It is, nevertheless, the truth.

I never led a more active life, or one more preoccupied even in inaction. I am writing, as you may probably know, an opera in four acts on a *libretto* by Scribe, called *La Nonne Sanglante.* It is based on the *Moine,* by Lewis, which you know. I do not imagine that this time any fault will be found with the piece by reason of any lack of interest in it. Scribe, in my opinion, has made the most of the famous legend; and he has, moreover, brought the drama to a close with a terrible *dénoûment,* borrowed from a work by M. de Kératry, and abounding in scenic effect.

They are counting upon me at the Opéra for this time next year; but Duprez is in such a state of vocal dilapidation that, if I cannot lay my hands on another leading tenor, it would be more than stupid on my part to produce my work. I have one in my eye, and I am superintending his education; he will make his first appearance next December in the *rôle* of Robert le Diable. I have great faith in him, but we must see him on the stage with the orchestra and the audience in front of him. He is called Delahaye, and he is a fine young fellow, whom I withdrew from studying medicine after I heard his lovely voice. He had everything to learn then, but he has made rapid progress. I have great hope of him. Time will show.

I had read an account of your agricultural success in the *Journal des Débats* before I received your letter. You have, I doubt not, founded a magnificent establishment; and, despite the natural advantages of your property, you must have worked hard and displayed much intelligent perseverance to have brought about such satisfactory results. You are a kind of Robinson Crusoe in your island, without the solitude or the savages. When the sun shines I am seized with a violent desire to set out on a visit to you, to inhale your perfumed breezes, to follow you through your fields, and to listen with you to the silence of your solitude. We understand each other so well, and my affection for you is so warm, so trustful, so undivided. But when the gloomy days return, the Paris fever claims me for its own, and I feel that to live elsewhere would be almost impossible. And yet, would you' believe it ? To the enthusiasm of my musical passion has succeeded a species of cold-bloodedness, resignation, contempt if you will, in regard to every obstacle I meet both in the practice and the contemporaneous history of art—obstacles which, by the way, have no terrors for me. On the contrary, the farther I go the more clearly I see that this eternal indifference enables me to husband the strength of which passion would deprive me. It is precisely the same with love; appear to fly, and you at once arouse a desire for pursuit.

You have doubtless heard of the *spaventoso* success which fell to the lot of my *Requiem* at St. Petersburg. It was performed from beginning to end at a concert given *ad hoc* by the full strength of all the lyric theatres and the choristers of the two regiments of the Imperial Guard, assembled together in the Czar's chapel. The performance, which was conducted by Henri Bomberg, was, according to the accounts given by those who heard it, incredibly majestic. Notwithstanding the pecuniary risks of such an undertaking, Bomberg cleared five thousand francs over and above the expenses, thanks to the generosity of the Russian nobility. Your despotic governments are, after all, the best supporters of art! Here, in Paris, I would not dream, even in my wildest moments, of producing this entire work unless I were prepared to lose as much as Bomberg gained.

Spontini has just returned. I wrote a letter to him at Berlin about the last performance of *Cortez*, which agitated me to such an extent that it brought on a nervous attack; it crossed him on the road. I have not seen him since his return for want of spare time to go as far as the Rue du Mail. I do not even know whether he has received my letter yet. He has been, so to speak, driven out of Prussia, and that was my reason for writing to him. In such a case one is bound to give utterance to every protest, however trivial, which can bring balm to the wounded heart of a man of genius, whatever may be his mental defects, and however great his egotism. The temple may possibly be unworthy the deity who dwells therein, but the deity is a deity for all that.

Our friend Gounet is in a sorry plight. By the failure of the notary, Lehon, he has lost almost all his mother's property and his own. He told me of this misfortune three months after the catastrophe took place. I never see Barbier now; it is more than six months since I met him.

This year, among other things, I have written the recitatives for Weber's *Der Freyschütz*, which I succeeded in producing at the Opéra without the slightest mutilation, correction, or *castil-blazade* of any kind, either in the words or the music. It is a marvellous masterpiece.

If you come this winter, we will have long talks about a thousand things which are almost incapable of explanation in a letter. I should so like to see you! It seems to me that I am going down hill with fearful velocity: life is so short, and the thought of its approaching end appears to have occurred to me very often for some time past, and so it comes to pass that I snatch with fierce avidity, rather than gather, the flowers within my reach as I glide down the slope of the bitter incline.

There has been, and there still is, some talk of bestowing upon me the post occupied by Habeneck at the Opéra; it would be a musical dictatorship, which, I hope, I should turn to the advantage of artistic interests; but before that can come to pass Habeneck must be removed to the Conservatoire, where Cherubini still slumbers. If I should grow old and incapable, I cannot fail to be appointed Director of the Conservatoire. I am still young, and consequently must not think about it.

LXXIII.

CÔTE-SAINT-ANDRÉ,
THURSDAY, SEPTEMBER 10, 1817.

MY DEAR HUMBERT,

I can only spare my father a week, so you see how impossible it is for me to pay you a visit. I leave on Sunday next, and shall be at Lyon on Monday morning. If by any chance you are there, or could manage to be there, I shall be opposite the post-office, Place Belle-court, at noon. I am very much annoyed at not having seen you. If I do not see you at Lyon, I will write you a less laconic epistle than this from Paris. I have never doubted either the interest you take in my doings, or your warm affection, which, as you know full well, I return with interest. I read, or rather I drank in, your pamphlet on Sardinia and the work of M. de la Marmora: it is admirably written, and displays a very rare rectitude of judgment and clearness of perception. I congratulate you heartily.

LXXIV.

NOVEMBER 1, 1817.

MY DEAR FRIEND,

I start the day after to-morrow for London, whither I am summoned, under most favourable conditions, to conduct the orchestra of the English Opera and to give four concerts. God only knows when we shall see each other again, my engagement being for six years, unless we chance to meet during the four months in the year when I shall be in Paris.

You have doubtless heard of the successful result of my trip to Russia, where my reception was quite imperial. Great success, large receipts, splendid performances, &c., &c.

My eyes now turn to England. France is becoming more and more profoundly stupid in all that relates to music. The more I look abroad the less I love my country. Pardon the blasphemy.

But art in France is dead, and mortification has set in. One must, therefore, go where it still lives. A singular revolution has apparently taken place in the musical sense of the English nation within the last ten years. We shall see.

LXXV.

JULY 8, 1850.

MY DEAR HUMBERT,

I was on the point of setting out for the Rue des Petits-Augustins when your letter arrived. I was going to tell you that your strophes are decidedly not couplets: that they express three sentiments too distinct and on too large a scale for a *song*, the music of which, if it is not to be execrable, should possess medium characteristics unworthy, in my opinion, of much consideration. The magnificent apostrophe to death, especially, possesses too much character to be relegated to a series of couplets. You have given me a poem, an ode, which needs Pindaric treatment. When I left you I felt that music stirring and clamouring within me; but its importance is so great that I cannot now devote myself to concentrating it. It is a question for a great composition, a chorus of men's voices and a powerful orchestra. I shall write it when we least expect it. I never was so wearily ill as I am now. I think of nothing but going to sleep; my head is always heavy, and an inexplicable feeling of uneasiness stupifies me. I need long, very long, journeys, and I cannot move further than from one bank of the Seine to the other.

Another thing, in strict confidence. Yesterday I read the passage about music in M. Mollière's book several times, and, to be quite frank, I shall have to combat three-fifths of his propositions. In spite of the explanations which he sent me through you, and which convict his style of a want of precision and clearness, I

208 THE LIFE AND LETTERS OF BERLIOZ.

discover that he has said very categorically, "Music may be defined as language rhythmically expressed and modulated by man."

No, it cannot be so defined.

Many other passages are calculated to give rise to endless controversies. Again, he says, by way of conclusion, "Performance also is realized by three methods, *major*, *minor*, and NATURAL."

What are the major and minor *methods* of performance? and what on earth is a *natural* method? It is positively past my comprehension.

The work is not one to be dismissed in a couple of lines, as one would treat a romance by Panseron, and I find myself so placed that I cannot possibly deal as I should wish with the portion devoted to music. You may believe me when I say that I am very sorry for it, and that I should have been delighted to have written an article, a really good one, to which the author and yourself are inclined to attach an importance which it would not in any case have possessed. It is a fact that whatever I write on such subjects is devoid of any value; it is not in my line. It would be just as reasonable to suppose that I could appreciate a Sanscrit poem.

Will you, my dear friend, call upon Gounet for me, and let me know how he is? His state of health makes me uneasy, and distresses me. Give my kind regards to Auguste.

LXXVI.

AUGUST 28, 1850.

My Dear Humbert,

There is nothing new here. The noble Assembly has risen for the vacation; we are almost destitute of representatives, and yet the sun continues to rise every day just as if the world was in perfect order. The newspapers persist in publishing contradictions on the subject of the reception accorded to the President in the provinces. What is true for one is false for another. " You are an ass ! " " You are another ! " And the reader is fain to say with Beaumarchais, *De qui se moque-t-on ici ?* Does not this nonsense appear to you very stupid and inordinately prolonged ?

The fact is, my dear fellow, that we have not yet been able to find the proper man to preside over the Republic. This worthy personage, very likely, is known, beloved, and respected. An upright and clever administrator, he is giving daily proofs of his right to that description by the remarkable manner in which he discharges the municipal functions entrusted to him during the last three years. He can already boast of having contributed to the well-being of thousands of ungrateful people, who forget him; he has ever exercised a powerful influence over the literary movement of our epoch; he is middle-aged, moderately ambitious, surfeited with glory, and proof against the seductions of popularity. In a word, he is a sage, a true philosopher. The Mayor of Courbevoie is the man; it is Odry !

The illustrious Mayor of Auteuil, M. Musard, has occasionally been spoken of with favour, but there is too much arrogance about him. He has involuntarily despised everything which has merely cleverness and good sense to boast of; he is a man of genius. People have done well, I think, in giving him up. But Odry, the brave and good Bilboquet! he is a necessity !

LXXVII.

HANOVER, NOVEMBER 13, 1853.

My DEAR HUMBERT,

I am writing to you on the mere chance of finding you, as I do not know whether you are at Belley, at Lyon, in Sardinia, or *in Europe.* I can only hope that my letter may reach you.

On my return from London in August I went to Baden to fulfil an engagement with M. Benazet, the proprietor of the gaming tables. There I organized and conducted a splendid festival, in the course of which we produced two acts of *Faust*, &c., &c. Thence I travelled to Frankfort, where I gave two more concerts in the theatre, still with *Faust*. There was no immense crowd as was the case at Baden, but I was *fêted* in a manner quite unusual in the *free towns;* that is to say, towns like Frankfort, which are slaves to mercantile ideas and *business*. After that I returned to Paris. I had scarcely settled down again when a twofold proposal reached me from Hanover and Brunswick, and off I started once more. To tell you of all the enthusiasm among the public and the artists of Brunswick would be too long a tale. A gold and silver *baton* presented by the orchestra; a supper of a hundred covers, at which all the talent of the town (imagine how they ate !), the Ministers of the Duke, and the musicians of the chapel, were present ; a charitable institution founded in my name (*sub invocatione sancti*, &c.) ; an ovation decreed by the populace one Sunday on the occasion of a performance of the *Carnaval Romain* at an open-air concert ; ladies kissing my hand in the street as they left the theatre ; anonymous wreaths sent to my house the same evening, &c., &c.

Yet another anecdote. On presenting myself at the first rehearsal the orchestra received me with trumpet blasts and applause, and I found my music covered with laurel branches as large as decent-sized legs. On the occasion of the last rehearsal the King and Queen appeared at 9 a.m., and remained until the end; in other words, until 1 p.m. At the concert, immense cheering, encores, &c. On the following day the King sent for me to ask me to give a second concert, which will take place the day after to-morrow.

"I did not believe," he said to me, " that any new beauty could be found in music; you have undeceived me. And how wonderfully you conduct ! I do not see you (the King is blind), but I feel it."

And when I dilated upon my good fortune in having such a *musician* to listen to me, he added,

"Yes, I owe much to Providence, which has granted me a sentiment for music by way of compensation for what I have lost."

These simple words, and the allusion to the double misfortune which befell the young King fifteen years ago, made a profound impression upon me.

I thought of you three weeks ago, when making a pedestrian tour among the Hartz Mountains, the scene of the orgy in *Faust*. I have never seen anything so beautiful; what forests, what torrents, what rocks! They are the ruins of a world. I looked for you in vain among those poetic summits. My emotion, I confess, overcame me.

Good-bye; write to me at the Poste-restante, Leipsic, until the 11th of next month.

This morning I received a visit from Madame d'Arnim, the Bettina of Goethe, who came, she said, not to *see me*, but *to look at me*. She is seventy-two and very clever.

LXXVIII.

SATURDAY MORNING, OCTOBER, 1854.

MY DEAR, MY VERY DEAR FRIEND,

I am really frightened by all the smiles lavished upon me by fortune during the last fortnight. You alone were wanting among my audience, and here you are!

It will take place to-morrow at two o'clock precisely, at Herz's, Rue de la Victoire. I send you two orders for the pit, so that you may be able to bring somebody with you, for I fear that you still need a supporting arm. I have no numbered stalls left, but you will be all right if you come early.

I would ask you to dine with me to-day, but my wife is so ill that I cannot manage it. You, perhaps, are still in ignorance of the fact that I married again two months ago.

I am overjoyed at the prospect of your hearing my new work.* It is an enormous success; the whole press, French, English, German, and Belgian, is singing loud hosannas in its praise, and there are two individuals here who are consumed with rage.

I must see you without fail to-morrow, after the concert.

LXXIX.

JANUARY 2, 1855.

MY DEAR, MY VERY DEAR FRIEND,

Your poem is admirable, superb, *magnificent*, as the English say; it affected me all the more on account of my son being in the Crimea. Poor boy, he was present at the taking of Bomarsund, and only passed through here on his way to join the fleet in the Black Sea. I was afraid at first of a satire after the manner of Hugo's *Chatiments !* Hugo madly furious at not being Emperor ! *Nil aliud !*

* *L'Enfance du Christ.*

But you reassured me very quickly; I am an ardent imperialist; I shall never forget that our Emperor rescued us from the filthy, stupid Republic! All civilized beings ought to remember that. He has the misfortune to be a barbarian in regard to art, but after all, he is a barbarian saviour, and Nero was an artist. There are minds of every hue.

Every day I am on the point of starting for Brussels. It is with great difficulty that I can attend to the preparations for the concert at the Théâtre-Italien, which is to take place at the end of this month.

I am engaged for three concerts in London, to produce *Roméo* and *Harold.* I do not know which way to turn. But I want to see you; make a definite appointment with me.

LXXX.

PARIS, NOVEMBER 3, 1858.

Oh, my poor, dear friend, how your letter has upset me! And I was accusing you of indifference towards me! I often said to myself, "Now that Ferrand has left Paris, he thinks of me no more; he merely condescends to let me know whether he is at Lyon, at Belley, or in Sardinia."

How I pity you, my dear friend! And yet,

according to your account, one ought to rejoice over the slight improvement in your health. You can think, you can write, you can walk. God grant that the severe winter with which we are threatened, and whose stings are already making themselves felt, may not retard the progress of your recovery.

As for me, I am a martyr to neuralgia, which for the last two years has settled in my intestines, and except at night, I am in constant suffering. When I was at Baden a short time ago, there were days when I could scarcely drag myself as far as the theatre to conduct the rehearsals. In a very few moments, however, the musical fever came to my assistance and restored my strength. I had to organize a grand performance of the first four parts of my *Roméo et Juliette* symphony. I had *eleven* desperate rehearsals. But what a performance it was! It was wonderful, and its success was extreme. The *Scène d'amour* (the *adagio*) drew forth copious tears, and I confess that nothing pleases me more than to produce this kind of music by means of music alone. Poor Paganini has never heard this work, composed specially for him.

We write to each other so seldom now, that I have to give you an account of my life during the last two years. This long time has been employed in the composition of an opera in five acts, the *Troyens*, of which, as in the case of *L'Enfance du Christ*, I have written both the words and the music. It is creating a great sensation almost everywhere; the English, German and even the French newspapers have said a great deal about it. I do not know what will become of this immense work, which at the present time has not the remotest chance of being performed. The Opéra is in confusion. It is, moreover, in some sense the Emperor's private theatre where no new works, except those by *clever* people, who manage to ingratiate themselves in one way or another. Well, it is finished; I have written it with an enthusiasm quite intelligible to you, who are so great an admirer of Virgilian inspiration.

Nobody knows anything about the music, but the *libretto*, which I have often read to crowded assemblies of artists and literary amateurs, is already looked upon in Paris as being something out of the common. I am sorry that I cannot let you make its acquaintance; by-and-bye I hope I shall be able to do so. It will undoubtedly be productive of considerable annoyance to me, but I have all along been prepared for that, and I shall put up with everything without a murmur.

Le Monde Illustré is publishing extracts from

my *Mémoires*, in which you are mentioned frequently. Has it come under your notice ?

Madame Ferrand has, doubtless, forgotten
me long ago. Will you recall me to her recollection and remember me very kindly to her.

You ask me for news of my son ; the dear
boy is a lieutenant on board a large French
vessel in the East Indies. He is on the eve of
returning.

LXXXI.

PARIS, NOVEMBER 8, 1858.

MY VERY DEAR FRIEND,

When I read your letters, so rich in
expressions of affection and dictated by so warm
and frank a heart, I think mine very cold and
very prosaic. But believe me, a species of
timidity makes me write thus ; I dare not give
my feelings full play, and I only half express
what I so thoroughly feel. Besides, I am convinced that you know it, so I will say no more.

I have received your burning poem, *Le
Brigand ;* it is very fine. It smells of powder
and newly cast bullets. But the article to
which you allude has not reached me. The
gaiety of this composition, which you compare
to flowerets entwining round a tombstone, is apparently the natural contrast between the subject discussed by certain spirits, and the minor

dispositions of the spirits themselves. I am often, as you were when you composed that, profoundly sad, even when assisting in a perfect firework display of human joy.

I am going to the office of *Le Monde Illustré* to order them to send you the numbers of that paper which contain extracts from my *Mémoires*. You will receive the remainder in due course as they appear. Although I have suppressed the most painful incidents (they will not see the light unless my son should publish the whole in volume form later on), the recital will, I fear, sadden you. But, possibly, you will like to be so saddened.

I will also send you, shortly, a complete score of *L'Enfance du Christ;* it appeared nearly three years ago. I dare not send you the *libretto* of the *Troyens*, as I have not sufficient confidence in the means of transit. But when I have some spare cash at my command, I will have it copied and will let it run the risk of a railway journey.

So your brother is with you? I thought he was far from Belley, though why I thought so is more than I can tell. Shake hands with him for me, and thank him for his kind message. What has become of our friend, Auguste Berlioz?

This morning I received a letter from Achille Paganini at Parma on the subject of my *Mémoires;* you will read it in *Le Monde Illustré* shortly. I received another letter this evening from Pisa, from a literary man who has sent me two operatic *librettos.* Alas! I am so constituted that the mere offer of a theme is enough to take away all desire, and frequently all possibility, of putting it to music.

Oh, how I wish I could read and sing **my** *Troyens* to you! There are some very curious things in it; at least, they seem so to me.

Heu! fuge nate deœ, teque his, ait, eripe flammis ;
Hostes habet muros, ruit alto a culmine Troja !

Ah! fuis, fils de Vénus! l'ennemi tient nos murs!
De son faite élevé Troie entière s'écroule !
    La mer de flamme roule,
Des temples au palais, les tourbillons impurs—
Nous eussions fait assez pour sauver la patrie
Sans l'arrêt du destin. Pergame te confie
Ses enfants et ses dieux. Va! . . . cherche l'Italie,
    Où, pour ton peuple renaissant,
Après avoir longtemps erré sur l'onde,
Tu dois fonder un empire puissant,
Dans l'avenir dominateur du monde,
    Où la mort des héros t'attend.

This recitative of Hector, brought to life for a moment by the will of the gods, but who gradually sinks into oblivion again as he accomplishes his mission to Æneas, is, I think, a strangely solemn and mournful musical idea. I quote this passage to you, because the idea in it is precisely one of those to which the public pays no attention.

LXXXII.

PARIS, NOVEMBER 19, 1858.

MY DEAR HUMBERT,

I had no thought even of contempt in regard to the anecdote of the Rue des Petits-Augustins and the lovely creature who wanted to open her window and listen to my humble trio. I like and admire the delicacy of your scruple, and I would embrace you heartily if I could for having expressed it. Oh, what an *ensemble* (to speak like the conductor of an orchestra) there is between us on certain points. It is evident that I was worthy of being your friend.

I have not forgotten anything in connection with the time you recall; but I am not writing my recollections any longer. They were all drawn up between 1848 and 1850, and I am merely publishing fragments of them so as to scrape together some money to pay for the course of study my son will have to go through at some seaport or other, on his return from India. *Auri pia fames!*

You will very shortly see the history of the *Francs Juges* in *Le Monde Illustré*. I could not forget that. As for the sapient critic who asserts that the overture to that opera should be classed as fantastic, I have not thought him worth the trouble of a reply; I have read many other silly statements just as well founded as that one is, but I shall never reply to any of them.

I called at the Ministry of State yesterday; the usher of the Minister showed me in without asking me if I had come by appointment, as he saw on my card, *Membre de l'Institut.* If I had not displayed that splendid title, I should have been shown the door without any ceremony. I had to speak to the Minister on the subject of the *Troyens* and the marked hostility of the Director of the Opéra against that work, of which he knows neither a line nor a note. His Excellency gave me all kinds of ambiguous assurances.

" Certainly—your great reputation—gives you a right—and fully justifies your pretensions.— But a grand opera in five acts—it is a terrible responsibility for a director—I will see about it —I have already had your work mentioned to me."

" But, sir, it is not a question of producing the *Troyens* this year or next; the Opéra is not in a condition to bring such an enterprise to a successful issue; you have not the necessary appliances; the Opéra in its present state is incapable of such an effort."

"Yes, but as a rule, compositions must be adapted to the means which do exist—at all events, I will think over it, and see what can be done."

And the Emperor himself is interested in it! He told me so, and within the last few days, I have had ample proof that he spoke the truth. And the President of the Council, and Count de Morny, both members of the Committee of the Opera, have read and heard my *libretto*, have pronounced it to be good, and spoke in my favour at the last meeting! And because the Opéra is managed by a semi-literary man, *who does not believe in musical expression*, and is of opinion that the words of the *Marseillaise* go as well to the air of *La Grâce de Dieu* as to that composed by Rouget de Lisle, I am to be kept at arm's length, very possibly for seven or eight years.

The Emperor is not sufficiently fond of music to interfere directly and energetically, and I shall be obliged to submit to the ostracism which this insolent theatre has from time immemorial pronounced against certain artists, without knowing the why or the wherefore. Mozart,

Haydn, Mendelssohn, Weber, and Beethoven were in the same plight; they all wished to write for the Paris Opéra, and not one of them was ever admitted to that honour.

Forgive me, my dear friend, for having made you a witness of my anger. Do not worry yourself about the means to be adopted in connection with the copying of the *Troyens;* I will manage it some day, sooner or later. In the meantime, I send you the full score of *L'Enfance du Christ;* you will, doubtless, prefer reading that to having the arrangement of it strummed on the piano, and by this means your recollections will be more easily awakened.

I leave you as I am interrupted. Besides, it is better so. I shall go out, and my nervous excitement will disappear.

LXXXIII.

November 26, 1858.

I have only one thing to say to you. I feel an absolute need of writing to you; why should I not give way to it? You will forgive me, will you not? I am ill and sad at heart. You see how many *I*'s I have managed to get into a few lines. What a pity it is! Always *I;* always *me;* no friend but *you;* and one ought to live only for one's friends.

Well, *I* am a brute, a leopard, a cat if you will; cats are sometimes really fond of their friends; I do not say their masters, because cats do not recognise masters.

The oppression on my heart decreases as I write to you; do not let us be, as we have been, years without writing to each other, I beseech you. We are dying with fearful rapidity; think of that. Your letters do me so much good. You have received the score of *L'Enfance du Christ*, have you not? There are no means of composing music here, where one ought to be rich like your friend Mirès. I was dreaming of it last night (of music, not of your friend Mirès). This morning my dream has come back to me; I performed it mentally, just as, three years ago at Baden, we performed the *adagio* out of Beethoven's symphony in B flat,

and growing wide awake by degrees, I fell into an unearthly ecstasy, and I shed all the tears of my soul as I listened to the sonorous smiles which shine from angels alone. Believe me, my dear friend, the being who wrote such a marvel of celestial inspiration was not a man. So must the archangel Michael sing, as he dreamingly contemplates the worlds uprising to the threshold of the empyrean. Oh, why have I not an orchestra under my hand, that I might sing this archangelic poem!

Let us come down to earth again. I am going to be disturbed—triviality, vulgarism, this stupid life! Away with an inspired orchestra! I should like to have a hundred pieces of ordnance wherewith to shoot all such things at once.

Good-bye; I am somewhat comforted. Forgive me!

LXXXIV.

PARIS, APRIL 28, 1859.

MY VERY DEAR FRIEND,

Ill as I am, I have still strength enough to rejoice greatly when I hear from you. Your letter has put new life into me. It took me by surprise, nevertheless, in the midst of the worry of a sacred concert which I gave last Saturday, the 23rd inst., in the theatre of the Opéra-Comique. *L'Enfance du Christ* was performed better than it has ever been. The choice of performers, vocal and instrumental, was excellent. You alone were wanting among the audience. The third part, the arrival at Saïf, produced a powerful emotional effect. The solo of the father of the family, *Entrez, pauvres Hébreux;* the trio of the young Israelites, and the conversation, *Comment vous nomme-t-on? Elle a pour nom Marie,* appeared to touch the audience excessively. The applause was unending. But, between ourselves, the part which produced a still greater effect was the mystic chorus at the end, *O mon âme,* which was played for the first time with the requisite shades and accent. The entire work is summed up in this vocal peroration. It seems to me to contain a feeling of the infinite, of divine love. I thought of you as I listened to it. My very dear friend, I cannot, as you can, give expression in my letters to certain sentiments common to us both, but I feel them, believe me. Besides, I dare not give myself up to them to too great an extent; there is so much flattery in what you write, so far as I am concerned. I am afraid of allowing myself to be influenced by your sympathetic words. Confess now, would it not be foolish of me to do so?

I had quite forgotten that you cannot have received *Le Monde Illustré* for several months past; forgive me. Are you a subscriber, as I see you still read it? If not, let me know, and I will send you the missing numbers and arrange for its regular transmission henceforth. It is a mere trifle, so do not think anything of it. The last numbers contain the account, very much diluted, of the offence against me attempted by Cavé and Habeneck on the occasion of the first performance of my *Requiem*. That part is creating a sensation. I frequently receive letters in prose and verse from my unknown friends, which console me.

In answer to your questions about the three new dramatic works of the present day, I must tell you that Gounod's *Faust* contains some very beautiful and some very indifferent numbers, and that some situations admirably adapted to musical effect are destroyed in the *libretto;* in fact, they would never have found them out if Goethe himself had not discovered them. The music of *Herculanum* is weak and *uncoloured* (pardon the neologism) to a degree! That of the *Pardon de Ploërmel*, on the other hand, is written in a masterly, ingenious, delicate, piquant, and frequently poetical manner.

There is a great gulf between Meyerbeer and these young people. One can see that he is not a Parisian. One sees quite the contrary as regards David and Gounod.

No, I have not taken any steps in connection with the *Troyens*. Nevertheless, it is attracting more and more attention. Véron, the ex-director, to whom I read the *libretto*, is passionately fond of the work, and goes about everywhere extolling what he is good enough to call " the poem." I let everybody talk and act as they please, and I remain as motionless as the mountain, waiting until Mahomet shall come to it.

I was at the Tuileries a fortnight ago; the Emperor saw me and shook hands with me. He is very favourably disposed towards me, but he has so many other battalions to command, that he very naturally cannot pay any attention to Greeks, Trojans, Carthaginians, and Numidians.

My coolness on the subject arises principally from my inability to find capable interpreters. The singers at the Opéra are so very far from possessing the qualifications necessary for acting, certain parts ! There is not among them a *Priameïa virgo*, a Cassandra. The Dido would be very inadequate to the *rôle*, and I would rather be stabbed ten times with a kitchen knife than hear the last monologue of the Queen of Carthage massacred.

> *Je vais mourir—*
> *Dans ma douleur immense submergée—*
> *Et mourir non vengée?*

As Shakespeare has said, nothing is more frightful than to see passion torn to tatters.

And passion abounds in the score of the *Troyens;* even the dead have a melancholy accent which seems to pertain somewhat to life; the young Phrygian sailor who, cradled on the top of the mast of a ship in the harbour of Carthage, weeps for the

> *Vallon sonore*
> *Où dès l'aurore,*
> *Il s'en allait chantant—*

is a victim to the most pronounced home-sickness; he passionately regrets Mount Didyma. He loves.

Another reply. I am going to Bordeaux in the first week in June for a charitable concert in which I am asked to conduct two scenes out of *Roméo et Juliette,* the *Fuite en Egypte,* and the *Carnaval Romain* overture.

In the month of August I shall return to Baden, and shall reproduce almost the whole of *Roméo et Juliette.* In order to perform the *finale,* I shall have to find a singer capable of successfully undertaking the part of Friar Laurence. In regard to the orchestra and the chorus, I shall be fully satisfied, I know. If you had heard last year how they sang the *adagio,* the love scene, and the balcony scene, that immortal scene which alone would suffice to make Shakespeare a demi-god! Ah, my dear friend, you might perhaps have said, as the Countess Kablergi did the day after the concert—

" It makes me weep still ! "

Am I not stupid ? You are too ill to think of moving ; otherwise, the trip to Baden in August would not be a very formidable affair. We should see each other at all events ! It is, more-over, a charming country ; lovely forests, burg-graves' castles, intellectual society, solitudes, to say nothing of the waters and the sun. But, after all, we are two impotent beings, and I have no right to complain when I reflect how much greater your sufferings are than mine. Good-bye, most noble brother. Let us be patient. Yours for ever.

LXXXV.

NOVEMBER 29, 1860.

MY DEAR FERRAND,

Thanks for your parcel. I have just read *Traître ou Héros?* It is vigorously written, very interesting, and full of local colour and warmth. In reply to your question, I reply unhesitat-ingly, that Ulloa was a traitor, and his action was infamous; his victory, due to lying and treachery, makes one's blood boil; if he refused money, he accepted distinctions, which, in his eyes, were equally valuable.   His motive was invariably the same, interest of one sort or another.   Would you believe that when I thought of the dagger of that brave Ephisio, the tears came to my eyes, and I gave a grunt like a savage.   Poor man! he killed the coward who abandoned his sister for filthy lucre, and he did well.   Next, he killed the judge who persecuted him, and again he did well.   But he did not kill his host, the man who stretched out the hand of friendship to him, and gave him food and shelter.   No, no, if there is a hero, it is Ephisio.

My dear friend, what is happening to you ? I heard of you from Pennet; he told me of your disappointments, your torments of every kind. If I have not written to you, I feel sure you have not put my silence down to indifference. I was embarrassed about alluding to the sad events you did not confide to me.   Now that you know that I am fully cognizant of everything, tell me if your more serious difficulties are smoothed away, and how your health is. As for me, I go up and down in the sad scale, but still I go forward.   I have just been seized with a fresh impulse for work, the result being a comic opera in one act, of which I have written the words and am finishing the music. It is gay and mirthful. There will be about a dozen musical numbers in it, which will rest me after the *Troyens*. Speaking of that great canoe which Robinson Crusoe cannot float, I must tell you that the theatre wherein my work is to be performed is approaching completion; but shall I find the people I need to sing it? That is the question. One of my friends has been to the Director of the Théâtre-Lyrique, who, we suppose, will be at the head of that administration next year also, to tell him that he will place fifty thousand francs at his disposal to assist him in producing the *Troyens* in a suitable manner. It is a great deal, but it is not all. So many things are needed for such a musical epopee.

Let me hear from you, I beseech you. How good it was of you to think of sending me your pamphlet! Remember me to your brother.

LXXXVI.

SUNDAY, JULY 6, 1861.

You are right, my dear friend. I ought to have written to you notwithstanding your long silence, because Pennet told me how painful it is to you to write even the shortest letter. But you must know that I, too, have been rudely shaken by an obstinate attack of neuralgia in the intestines. There are days when I cannot even write ten lines consecutively. It occasionally takes me four days to finish an article. I am not in so much pain to-day, and I take advantage of that circumstance to reply to your questions.

Yes, the *Troyens* is accepted at the Opéra by the Director, but the *mise en scène* now depends upon the Minister of State. It so happens that Count Walewski, good-natured and gracious as he has been to me, is at the present moment very much put out because I refused to conduct the rehearsals of *Alceste* at the Opéra. I declined that honour on account of the transpositions and alterations necessary to adapt the part to Madame Viardot's voice. This sort of thing is quite incompatible with the opinions I have professed throughout my life. But Ministers, and especially Ministers of the present day, do not understand such artistic scruples, and will not put up with the slightest opposition to any of their wishes. For the time being, therefore, I do not stand well at Court, a circumstance which does not prevent the musical world of Germany and Paris doing me justice.

I shall only be present at a few of the rehearsals,
and shall give the stage manager the benefit of
my advice, in order to prove to the Minister
that I am not obstructive. The Director thinks
that this show of amiability will suffice to charm
away the ill-humour of Count Walewski.

First of all, an opera in five acts by Gounod,
which is not finished yet, is to be produced;
then another one by Gevaert, a Belgian composer but little known, after which they will
probably set to work on the *Troyens*. Public
opinion and the whole of the press support me
so strongly that there is scarcely any possibility of opposition. I have, moreover, made
an important alteration in the first act in deference to the wish of Royer, the Director. The
work is now precisely the length to which he
wished it to be reduced; I have been most pliant
throughout the whole business, and have consequently only to fold my arms and wait until
my two rivals shall have done their part. I am
thoroughly resolved to torment myself no more;
I am no longer running after fortune, but awaiting it in bed.

I, however, could not help replying somewhat too frankly, perhaps, to the Empress,
who asked me at the Tuileries a few weeks ago
when she was likely to hear the *Troyens*.

" I do not quite know, madame, but I am beginning to think that one must live a hundred years to be performed at the Opéra."

The worst of these delays is that the work is being credited with a premature reputation which may detract from its success. I have read the *libretto* almost everywhere, and fragments of the score were heard two months ago at M. Edouard Bertin's. It has been much talked about, and this makes me anxious.

In the meantime I am having the score for voice and piano stereotyped, not with the design of publishing it, but in order that it may be ready when the time for its performance shall arrive. Do you know to whom I have dedicated it? The title-page was brought to me yesterday; it bears on the face of it these two words: *Divo Virgilio.*

I assure you, my dear friend, that it is written in a good style, grandly simple. I am speaking of the musical style. I shall be rejoiced beyond measure when I can make you hear at all events a few scenes. But how is that to be done?

The point at issue now is, who among the ladies of our vocal Olympus are to play the parts of Cassandra and Dido? In addition to this, I am at my wits' end to find a tenor and baritone for Æneas and Chorœbus.

I am gradually finishing a comic opera in one act for the new theatre at Baden, the building of which is rapidly approaching completion. I have based this act on Shakespeare's comedy, *Much Ado about Nothing*.

It is simply called *Béatrice et Bénédict*, and I can, at all events, answer for it that it does not contain *much ado*. Benazet, the king of Baden, will produce it next year, if I can hit upon an opportune moment, which is doubtful. We shall get our artists from Paris and Strasburg. A woman with plenty of spirit is needed for Beatrice? Is one to be found in Paris?

I shall leave for Baden a month hence to organize and conduct the annual festival. This time I shall let them have the fragments of the *Requiem*, the *Tuba mirum*, and the *Offertorium*. I want to indulge my own inclination so far, and after all there is no great harm in making all those rich idlers bestow a thought or two upon death.

LXXXVII.

JULY 14, 1861.

Alas! my dear friend, a visit to you, and the mutual refreshing of mind and heart which would be attendant on it, is a luxury beyond even my dreams. I am a slave, as you are in your circle, to business, labours, and innumerable obligations, *siam servi*, if not *agnor frementi*, as Alfieri says, at all events sad and resigned.

I have received the new copy of *Traître ou Héros?* and will make Philarète Chasles read it; he will be able to mention it in the *Journal des Débats*, and in case he does not write anything about it, I will try Cuvillier-Fleury, who also has a speciality for such subjects. As far as I am concerned, I will allude to it in one of my articles the first time I have an opportunity of so doing.

You have not sent me your *Puissance des nombres*. Michel Lévy would be the best publisher for such a work. When you want me to speak to him, give me ample details about it, and let me know whether it will consist only of contributions already published in the newspapers. That is the first question he will ask.

From the 6th to the 28th of August I shall be at Baden, where you can write to me, simply addressing the letter to me by my name without the addition of any street. My son, about whom you are good enough to inquire, is at this moment in the neighbourhood of Naples. He is one of the officers on board a vessel belonging to the Messageries Impériales. He has passed his examination for the rank of navigating captain, and expects to sail for China shortly.

An American *impresario* made me an offer to go to the dis-United States this year, but it came to nothing by reason of certain antipathies which I cannot overcome, and the absence in me of any great greed for gain. I do not know if your love for this great nation and its utilitarian manners is any keener than mine. I doubt it.

Moreover, I could not prudently absent myself from Paris for a year. I may be asked for the *Troyens* from one moment to another. If any serious accident should happen at the Opéra, they would necessarily fall back upon me. If I were absent I should be in the wrong.

LXXXVIII.

JULY 27, 1861.

MY DEAR FRIEND,

I am writing to you to-day because I have a leisure moment, which I should, possibly, have considerable difficulty in finding to-morrow or the day after.

Michel Lévy is absent from Paris. So, not to lose any time, I called on M. Bourdilliat, the manager of the *Librairie Nouvelle*, and offered him the business, handing him at the same time the manuscript note you sent me, and a copy of *Traître ou Héros?* which I asked him to read. He seemed disposed to accept your proposal, and will reply and let me know his terms on Monday next. He published my *Grotesques de la Musique.* I hope to succeed for you.

Good-bye; I will write you more at length next week, before I leave for Baden.

LXXXIX.

FRIDAY, AUGUST, 1861.

MY DEAR FERRAND,

After three appointments missed, not by me, M. Bourdilliat has given me an evasive answer, which is equivalent to a refusal. Michel Lévy has not returned; he will, no doubt, be in Paris when I come back from Baden, and I will then see what I can do with him.

I am so ill to-day that I have no strength to write any more. All this worries me as such absurdities must worry one. I start next Monday.

XC.

FEBRUARY 8, 1862.

MY DEAR HUMBERT,

I am answering you in haste, first of all to thank you for your friendly remembrance of me, and then to give you in a few lines the information you want.

Is it a fact that I have not written to you since my return from Baden? I cannot understand it. Yes, the concert was superb, and I heard *our* symphony, *Harold*, played for the first time as I would have it played. The fragments of the *Requiem* produced a terrific effect, but we had eight rehearsals.

I received your little book, *Jacques Valperga*, and I read it with lively interest, in spite of the scant sympathy with which its sadly historical personages inspire me.

I am somewhat less unwell than usual, thanks to a rigid diet which I have adopted.

The Minister of State is in a healthy state of mind so far as I am concerned; he wrote me a letter of thanks in connection with the *mise en scène* of *Alceste*, the rehearsals of which I conducted at the Opéra. At last he has given Royer orders to commence the study of the *Troyens* after the opera of the Belgian, Gevaert, which will be produced next September. I shall, consequently, witness a performance of mine in March, 1863. In the meanwhile, I am having weekly rehearsals at home of the opera in two acts which I have just completed for the new theatre at Baden. *Béatrice et Bénédict* will be produced at Baden on the 6th of August next. As in the case of the *Troyens*, I have written the words, and I am a prey to an unwonted torment, that of hearing my dialogue *spoken* in a manner opposed to common-sense; but by dint of coaching my actors I think I shall succeed in making them speak like men.

XCI.

PARIS, JUNE 30, 1862.

MY DEAR FERRAND,

I am writing you merely a few lines in my desolation. My wife has just died with awful suddenness from heart disease. No words of mine can describe the fearful isolation which has resulted from this sudden and violent separation. Forgive me for not writing more.

XCII.

PARIS, AUGUST 21, 1862.

MY DEAR HUMBERT,

I have just returned from Baden, where my opera *Béatrice et Bénédict* has achieved a signal success. The French, German, and Belgian papers are unanimous in extolling it. Whatever befalls me, be it good or bad, I am always in a hurry to tell you all about it, assured

as I am of the affectionate interest with which
you will receive the news. Unfortunately you
were not there; the performance would have recalled that of the *Enfance du Christ* to your
memory. The opposition and abusive clique
stayed in Paris. A great number of writers and
artists, on the contrary, undertook the journey.
The performance, which I conducted, was excellent, and Madame Charton-Demeur, the
Beatrice, in particular had moments of veritable
inspiration both as a singer and an actress.
Well, you will scarcely believe me when I tell
you that I was suffering so terribly from my
neuralgia that I took no interest in anything,
and I ascended my *rostrum*, in face of the
Russian, German, and French crowd, to conduct the first performance of an opera of which
I had written both words and music, without
the least emotion. The result of this eccentric
coolness was that I conducted better than
usual. I was far more uneasy at the second
performance.

Bénazet, who invariably does everything on a
large scale, spent an immense sum of money
upon the dresses, scenery, actors, and chorus
for the opera. He made a point of inaugurating
the new theatre splendidly. It is making a
tremendous sensation here. They wanted to

produce *Béatrice* at the Opéra-Comique, but there was no Beatrice to be had. In our theatres there is not a single woman capable of singing and acting this part, and Madame Charton-Demeur is on the point of leaving for America.

You would laugh if you could read all the silly praises bestowed upon me by the critics. They are discovering that I have the gift of melody, that I am gay, and even comic. The history of the astonishment caused by the *Enfance du Christ* is repeating itself. They have come to the conclusion that I am not noisy because they do not see any blaring instruments in the orchestra. What an amount of patience I should need if I were not so indifferent!

My dear friend, I suffer martyrdom *every day* now, from 4 a.m. till 4 p.m. What is to become of me? I do not tell you this to make you bear your own sufferings patiently; I know full well that mine do not afford you any compensation. I cry aloud to you as one is always tempted to cry to beings loving and beloved.

XCIII.

PARIS, AUGUST 26, 1862.

Your letter, my dear friend, which has just arrived, has done me a world of good. Thank

Madame Ferrand for her pressing invitation to me to be near you. I stand in so much need of seeing you that I should have set out at once, did not a mass of paltry bonds keep me here at present. My son has resigned the post he held on board a ship belonging to the Messageries Impériales, and from what my friends in Marseilles say, he was right in doing so. He is now cast adrift, and it becomes necessary to look out for some fresh employment for him. I have other matters to attend to, consequent on the death of my wife. In addition to these, I have to see after the publication of the score of *Béatrice,* as I am slightly enlarging the musical portion of it in the second act. I am engaged in writing a trio and a chorus, and I cannot leave the work in suspense. I am in a hurry to untie or cut all the bonds which chain me to art, so that I may be at any time ready to say to death, " Whenever you please! " I dare not complain when I think of your intolerable sufferings, and the aphorism of Hippocrates may fitly be applied to our case ; *Ex duobus doloribus simul abortis vehementior obscurat alterum.* Are such sufferings the compulsory consequences of our organizations? Must we be punished for having throughout our lives adored the beautiful? Probably so. We have drunk too deeply of the intoxicating cup; we have run too far after the ideal.

How beautiful are your verses on the swan! I took them for a quotation from Lamartine!

You, my dear friend, you have an attentive and devoted wife to aid you in bearing your cross! You have no knowledge of the terrible duet sung in your ears, during the busy whirl of day and amid the silence of the night, by weariness and isolation! God keep you from the knowledge of it, for it is sorry music!

Good-bye; the tears which well up to my eyes would make me say things that would only render you more melancholy still. But I am going to try to free myself, and I will not fail to pay you a visit, even though it should be a short one and in the winter time. I have no need of the sun; the sun shines always where I can see you.

XCIV.

SUNDAY, NOON, FEBRUARY 22, 1863.

MY DEAR HUMBERT,

I hasten to reply to your letter, which afforded me a moment of unexpected joy this morning. I am going immediately to conduct a concert in which, for the second time within a fortnight, the *Fuite en Egypt* and other compositions of mine are to be performed. At the first performance the little oratorio drew forth transports of tears, and the manager of the concerts asked me to repeat the entire programme to-day. I shall miss you sadly among the audience.

I am going to answer your questions in a few words, I have broken with the Opéra once and for all in regard to the *Troyens*, and I have accepted the proposals of the Director of the Théâtre-Lyrique. He is now hard at work getting the company, orchestra, and chorus together. The rehearsals will begin next May, so that we may be able to produce the work in December.

Béatrice is stereotyped, and I will send you a copy. On the 1st of April I shall leave for Weimar, where the Grand Duchess has asked me to produce the opera on the occasion of her birthday. In August we shall bring it out again at Baden. In June I shall go to Strasburg to conduct the festival of the Lower Rhine, for which the *Enfance du Christ*, the entire work, is being studied.

I am still very unwell; my neuralgia has become intensified to a pitch beyond my powers of description, in consequence of a frightful annoyance to which I have again been subjected.

For the last week I have been utterly incapable of writing to you. I am beginning to regain my strength, and I shall survive this fresh trial. My heart is torn within me.

My friends, male and female, appear to have come to a fortunate determination to surround me with care and delicate attention, though they know nothing about the matter, and Providence has sent me some music to compose.

A fortnight hence the duet from *Béatrice*, *Nuit Paisible et Sereine*, is to be sung at a concert at the Conservatoire, and I shall once more be face to face with the audience who were so enthusiastic the other day. I have a delicious tenor also who sings *Les Pélerins Étant Venus* admirably.

I have received your packet, and I read with avidity the details about the isthmus of Suez. What a *fête* the opening of the canal will be!

Good-bye, my dear friend; I have only just time to dress. The orchestra rehearsal yesterday was excellent; I believe the performance will be superb. I embrace you with all that remains of my heart.

XCV.

MARCH 3, 1863.

You did well, my dear friend, to send me your manuscript. I will do what you ask me, and right heartily, I assure you. Your conjectures on the subject of my distress are, happily, erroneous. Alas! my poor Louis has tormented me cruelly, but I have forgiven him so completely! We have both of us carried out your programme. This annoyance came to an end three months ago. Louis is once more on board ship, and expects to be captain soon. He is now in Mexico, on the point of sailing for France, where he expects to arrive a month hence.

It is a question of love once more, a love which came upon me in smiling guise, which I never sought, but, on the contrary, even resisted for some time. The state of isolation in which I live, and the inexorable need of tenderness which kills me, conquered in the end; I allowed myself to love, my love increased a hundred fold, and a voluntary separation on both sides then became necessary and compulsory. A separation complete, without compensation, absolute as death itself. There you have the whole story. I am being gradually restored to health, but health under the circumstances is so sad. Do not let us talk about it any more.

I am very glad my *Béatrice* pleases you. I am on the eve of setting out for Weimar, where it is being studied now. I shall conduct a few

performances of the opera there in the beginning
of April, and shall afterwards return to this
desert, Paris. The duet, *Nuit paisible*, was to
have been sung at the Conservatoire next Sunday, but my two vocalists write to ask me to
postpone it until the concert of the 28th, and I
cannot do otherwise than consent.

At the present time I should be very anxious
about the arrival of my Dido if I could ever feel
anxiety any more. Madame Charton-Demeur
is at sea, on her return from Havannah, and I
do not know whether she has accepted the terms
offered her by the Director of the Théâtre-
Lyrique ; without her the performance of the
Troyens is an impossibility. Well, who lives
will see. But the Cassandra? I am told she
has both a voice and dramatic feeling. She is
still at Milan ; she is a Madame Colson, whom
I do not know. How will she render that air
which Madame Charton sings so well ?—

> *Malheureux roi! dans l'éternelle nuit,*
> *C'en est donc fait, tu vas descendre.*
> *Tu ne m'écoutes pas, tu ne veux rien comprendre,*
> *Malheureux peuple, à l'horreur qui me suit.*

But Madame Charton cannot play both parts,
and that of Dido is still more important and
more difficult. Pray, my dear friend, that my
indifference on every subject may become complete, for I shall have to suffer cruelly if I give
way to any depth of feeling during the eight or

nine months preparatory to the production of the *Troyens*.

Good-bye; when, on getting up in the morning, I see your dear handwriting awaiting me, I am cheered for the remainder of the day. Do not forget that.

XCVI.

MARCH 30, 1863.

MY DEAR HUMBERT,

I have only time to thank you for your letter, which I have just received. I start immediately for Weimar, and besides, I am in such terrible agony that I can scarcely write. I hope to be able to send you good news of the German *Béatrice*. The manager wrote to me three days ago to say that everything was going on well.

Last Sunday, at the sixth Conservatoire concert, Madame Viardot and Madame Van Denheuvel sang the duet *Nuit paisible* before the public here, so hostile to living composers and so full of prejudice. Its success was overwhelming; it was encored amid the applause of the entire audience. During its repetition there was an interruption, caused by the emotion of some ladies at the passage,

Tu sentiras couler les tiennes à ton tour
Le jour où tu verras couronne ton amour.

That creates an incredible sensation.

I am leaving the Director of the Théâtre-Lyrique busy in making the necessary engagements for the *Troyens*. The absurd terms demanded by our Dido are stopping the way.

The Cassandra is engaged.

My God, how I suffer! And I have not time even for that.

XCVII.

WEIMAR, APRIL 11, 1863.

MY DEAR FRIEND,

Béatrice has achieved a signal success here. After the first performance I was complimented by the Grand Duke and the Grand Duchess, and especially by the Queen of Prussia, who was at a loss to know how to express her delight.

Yesterday I was twice summoned before the curtain, after the first and second acts. When the performance was over I went to supper with the Grand Duke, who overwhelmed me with civilities of every kind. He is really an incomparable Mæcenas. He has arranged a private entertainment for to-morrow, when I am to read the *libretto* of the *Troyens*. The artists of Weimar, and those who have come from the neighbouring towns, and even from Dresden and Berlin, presented me with a huge bouquet.

I start to-morrow for Lowenberg, whither the Prince of Hohenzollern has invited me to conduct a concert with a programme of his own arranging, and composed of my overtures and symphonies. I shall then return to Paris, where I hope to hear from you.

Shall I find the *Troyens* in rehearsal? I doubt it. When I absent myself everything comes to a standstill.

I shall be very pleased to receive a pretty little volume, *Traître ou Héros?* Will it be ready soon?

In the midst of my rejoicing last night I took the liberty of embracing my Beatrice, who is charming. She was rather surprised at first, but afterwards she looked me full in the face, and said, "Oh! I must embrace you too!"

If you only knew how well she sings her

I have heard much praise bestowed on the translator's work, but in spite of my ignorance of the German language, I have detected a great want of faithfulness in very many places. His excuses are very lame, and irritate me. He is the same man who translated my book, *A Travers Chants*. For instance, in the passage

" This *adagio* seems to have been breathed forth by the Archangel Michael one evening when, in a melancholy mood, he contemplated the worlds uprising to the threshold of the empyrean," he has taken the Archangel Michael to mean Michael Angelo, the great Florentine painter. I leave you to imagine the stupid nonsense which such a substitution of persons makes of the German translation ! Is not that enough to make one hang such a translator? But, after all, he is so thoroughly devoted to me, and such an excellent fellow.

God keep you from seeing your *Héros* translated ; he would be turned into a traitor, and your *Traître* into a hero.

Do your best to let me find a letter from you lying on my table when I get back.

XCVIII.

Paris, May 9, 1863.

My Dear Friend,

I arrived here ten days ago. I received your letter this morning, and was going to sit down to reply to you at length—I have so many things to say to you—when I was obliged to go to the Institut. I have come back very tired and in great suffering. I am only going to send you a line or two, and then I shall retire

to bed until six o'clock. Have I told you about
my pilgrimage to Lowenberg and the performance of my symphonies by the Prince of Hohenzollern's orchestra? I forget.

On the morning of my departure the good
Prince said, as he embraced me, "You are
going back to France, and you will meet there
people who love you. Tell them I love them."

I was completely upset on the day of the
concert, when, after the *adagio*, the love scene,
in *Roméo et Juliette*, the Chapel-master, who was
in tears, exclaimed in French, "No, no, no,
there is nothing more beautiful than that!"
Then the orchestra stood up. There was a blast
of trumpets and a shout of applause. I seemed
to see the smiling countenance of Shakespeare
beaming upon me, and I longed to say, "Father,
are you content?"

I think I have already told you all about the
success of *Béatrice* at Weimar.

No commencement even has yet been made
in connection with the *Troyens*. A money difficulty stops everything. As you are so anxious
to become acquainted with this ponderous score,
I cannot resist the temptation of sending it to
you. I have, therefore, this morning sent a
clean proof to be bound, and you shall have it
a week or ten days hence. No, the action does

not pass altogether at Troy. It is written on the plan adopted by Shakespeare in his historical plays, and you will find in the *denoûment* the sublime, *Oculisque errantibus alto, quæsivit cælo lucem ingemuitque repertâ.* I will only ask you, my dear friend, not to allow this copy to go out of your hands, the work not having yet been published.

I leave on the 15th of June for Strasburg, where I am going to conduct the *Enfance du Christ* at the festival of the Lower Rhine on the 22nd. On the 1st of August I shall be off once more to Baden, where we are going to reproduce *Béatrice.*

The Prince of Hohenzollern presented me with his cross. The Grand Duke of Weimar insisted on writing a letter on my behalf to the Duchess of Hamilton for the express purpose of having it brought under the notice of the Emperor. The letter has been read. I was summoned to the Ministry; I spoke out frankly, glossing nothing over, nor dealing merely in set phrases, and I compelled them to acknowledge that I was right, and—there the matter will rest. The poor Grand Duke! He cannot understand a sovereign being devoid of interest in art! He scolded me severely for not wishing to write any more.

"The good God," he said, "in giving you such talent, did not mean you to leave it unemployed."

He made me read the *Troyens* one evening at Court in the presence of a score of people who understood French thoroughly. It made a deep impression.

Good-bye, my dear friend; remember me to Madame Ferrand and your brother. I am ill and greedy of sleep.

XCIX.

Paris, June 4, 1863.

My Dear Friend,

I fear I have overtaxed your strength, for I see very clearly, by your tremulous handwriting, that your hand is not as steady as it used to be. Let me beg of you, therefore, to refrain from sending me lengthy remarks about my musical attempts. You might as well write articles, and I know what that means, even when you are in good health and spirits; *miseris succurrere disco*. I shall be satisfied if I can distract your attention for a moment from your sufferings.

Carvalho and I are at length fairly harnessed to that huge machine, the *Troyens*. I read the piece three days ago to the assembled company at the Théâtre-Lyrique, and the rehearsals of the choruses are to begin forthwith. The negotiations entered into with Madame Charlton-Demeur have been brought to a successful issue; she is engaged to play the part of Dido, and the news has caused a great sensation in the musical world of Paris. We hope to be ready by the beginning of December, but I have been obliged to give my consent to the performance of the last three acts only. They will be divided into five, and preceded by a prologue which I have just completed, the theatre being neither rich enough nor large enough to put the *Prise de Troie* on the stage. Later on we shall see if the Opéra will be inclined to give the *Prise de Troie*.

C.

PARIS, JUNE 27, 1863.

MY DEAR FRIEND,

I have returned from Strasburg crushed and overcome. *Enfance du Christ*, performed before a perfect multitude, created a stupendous effect. The room, constructed *ad hoc* in the Kléber Square, contained eight thousand five hundred people, and yet every note was heard throughout the building. The audience wept, applauded, and involuntarily interrupted several movements. You can have no idea of the impression produced by the mystic chorus at the end, *O mon âme!* In it I saw the religious ecstasy of which I have dreamt, and which I have felt while writing. An unaccompanied chorus sung by two hundred men and two hundred and fifty women who had been rehearsing for three months! They did not go down even half a quarter of a tone. Such a thing is unknown in Paris. At the last *Amen*, the *pianissimo* which seems to lose itself in the mysterious distance, a burst of applause broke forth such as I never heard; sixteen thousand hands were applauding together. Then came a deluge of flowers and manifestations of every kind. I looked for you in the crowd.

I was very ill, and very much weakened by my neuralgic pains; one must pay for everything in this world. How are you? Your last letter gave me the impression that you were in great suffering. Let me have *three lines* from you.

I am now in the thick of the double study of *Béatrice* and the *Troyens*. Madame Charlton-Demeur is so enraptured with the part of Dido that she lies awake at night thinking of it. May the gods sustain and inspire her! *Di morientis Elyssæ!* But I never cease repeating to her,

"Do not be afraid of any of my bold flights, and do not cry."

In spite of Boileau's advice, to save me from tears none must be shed.

P.S.—I shall be at Baden for the reproduction of *Béatrice* from the 1st to the 10th of August, and I shall be *very much alone*. If you are strong enough, you would be doing an act of piety by sending me a few lines to the Post-restante there.

My director, Carvalho, has at last succeeded in obtaining a subsidy of a hundred thousand francs. He can go on fearlessly now. His painters, decorators, and chorus-singers are at work : his enthusiasm for the *Troyens* increases. The year has been bright ever since it began; will it go on thus to the end? Pray that it may be so.

CI.

JULY 8, 1863.

My DEAR FRIEND,

It is not my fault; my conscience is quite clear on the subject of the trouble you took to write me so long and so eloquent a letter. I myself begged you to do nothing of the kind. To write articles without being driven to it! And ill and suffering as you are! But fortunately, I have nothing more to send you. I received the little, too little, volume of *Ephisio*. I will take it with me to Baden, so that I may present it to Théodore Anne if I meet him. In fact, he is in a position to write something about it which will be of great assistance to you. You can send me another copy. I should like to see Cuvillier-Fleury review *Traître ou Héros?* in the *Journal des Débats*, but he is one of the unget-at-able kind. It is nearly a year since I saw him last; he is very rarely in Paris. The *Journal des Débats* is exceedingly contemptuous towards me, and scarcely ever alludes to anything in connection with me.

I am only writing you these few words to scold you for having said so many pretty things to me. I leave you now to go and hear my *Anna soror** rehearse ; she is a source of considerable anxiety to me. She is young and pretty, and has a magnificent contralto voice, but she is the incarnation of anti-music, if there is any such extraordinary species of monster in existence. I have to teach her everything, note by note, over and over again. I must infuse a little style into her in anticipation of a rehearsal with Madame Charton-Demeur which is to take place at my house in a few days. Dido would be angry if

* Mademoiselle Dubois.

her *soror* did not know her part of the duet, *Reine d'un jeune empire*, which she herself sings so admirably. After that is over, Carvalho and I are going to call upon Flaubert, the author of *Salammbô*, to consult him about Carthaginian costumes.

Do not inflict any regrets upon me. I must resign myself to my fate. There is no Cassandra now; the *Prise de Troie* will not be given, and, for the time being, the first two acts are suppressed. I have been obliged to replace them by a prologue, and the scene will open in Carthage. The Théâtre-Lyrique is neither rich enough nor large enough, in addition to which the entire work would last too long. Besides, I could not find a Cassandra.

Mutilated as it is, the work, divided into five acts and the prologue, will last from eight o'clock until midnight, on account of the complicated scenery of the virgin forest and the final *tableau*, the funeral pile and the apotheosis of the Roman Capitol.

CII.

PARIS, JULY 24, 1863.

MY DEAR FRIEND,

I saw M. Theodore Anne a few days ago; I mentioned your book to him, and he promised me that he would write an article on it in the *Union*. I, consequently, took him the volume. We have now to see if he will keep his word. Do you read the *Union* regularly? I will also speak to Cuvillier-Fleury as soon as I can catch him. I will give him the other copy of *Traître ou Héros?*, which has been sent back to me.

Good-bye; I am going to have a rehearsal here immediately with my three songstresses, and have only time to shake you by the hand. I shall not leave for Baden until the 1st of August.

CIII.

TUESDAY, JULY 28, 1863.

What a splendid institution the post is! For four *sous* we can have a chat, however far away we are from each other. Can anything be more charming?

My son arrived yesterday from Mexico, and as he has managed to get leave of absence for three weeks, I shall take him with me to Baden. The poor boy never happens to be in Paris when any of my works are being performed. The only complete performance he has ever heard was one of the *Requiem*, when he was twelve years old. You may imagine his delight

at the prospect of seeing two performances of
Béatrice. After leaving Baden he will sail for
Vera-Cruz, but he will be back again in November
for the first night of the *Troyens*.

No, there is no question about rehearsing the
trio, *Je vais d'un cœur aimant;* that is known
perfectly. It is a question of working at the
Troyens, and to-day I had Dido, Anna, and
Arcanius with me. These ladies know their
parts now, but the daily rehearsals by the whole
company will not begin for a month yet. I
have sold the score to Choudens, the publisher,
for fifteen thousand francs. This sale in
advance is a good sign.

Madame Charton will be a superb Dido. She
sings the whole of the last act admirably, and
in certain passages, such as this for instance,

Esclave, elle l'emporte en l'éternelle nuit !

she will wring all hearts.

Her only fault lies in certain notes which
have a tendency to become flat when she
attempts any gradations in the *pianissimo*
passages, and I am doing my utmost to prevent
her from introducing any such effects, too
dangerous for her voice.

I have made enemies of two friends, Madame
Viardot and Madame Stoltz, who both aspired
to the throne of Carthage. *Fuit Troja*, but

singers persist in ignoring the irreparable havoc produced by time.

Good-bye, my dear friend. I start on Sunday.

CIV.

SUNDAY MORNING, OCTOBER, 1863.

Your letter has arrived, and I have barely time to tell you that the rehearsals of the *Troyens* are a complete success. Yesterday I was so thoroughly overcome when I left the theatre that I could scarcely speak or walk. In all probability I shall not be in a fit state to write to you on the evening of the performance. I shall have lost my head completely.

CV.

THURSDAY, NOVEMBER 5, 1863.

Splendid success; profound emotion on the part of the audience, tears, interminable applause, and *a hiss* at the end when I was called for by name. The septet and the *duo d'amour* convulsed the whole room; the septet was encored. Madame Charton was superb; she is a veritable queen; she was transformed; nobody had any idea that she possessed such dramatic talent. I am almost stunned with so much embracing. Your hand alone was wanting.

CVI.

NOVEMBER 10, 1863.

MY DEAR HUMBERT,

Later on I will send you a bundle of papers containing notices of the *Troyens*: I am studying them. The immense majority of them bestow unqualified praise on the author.

The third performance took place yesterday, with even more perfect *ensemble* and effect than the preceding ones. The septet was again encored, and a portion of the audience wanted to hear the *duo d'amour* over again, but it was too late to repeat it. In the last act, Dido's air, *Adieu, fière cité*, and the chorus of the priests of Pluto, which one of my critics calls the *De Profundis de Tartare*, produced an immense sensation. The pathos of Madame Charton was admirable. To-day I am just beginning, like the Queen of Carthage, to recover my *calm* and *serenity*. All these anxieties and fears have shattered me. I have no voice left, and can scarcely speak two words aloud.

Good-bye, my dear friend; my joy becomes twofold when I remember that it is yours also.

CVII.

THURSDAY, NOVEMBER 26, 1863.

MY DEAR HUMBERT,

I am still confined to my bed. My bronchitis is obstinate, and I cannot be present at the performance of my work. My son goes every other day and brings me an account of the events of the evening. I lack courage to send you the ever-increasing mass of newspapers. You have, doubtless, read Kreutzer's superb article in the *Union*. I am at this moment in treaty with the manager of Her Majesty's Theatre in London. He came over to hear the *Troyens*, and was honest enough to make no secret of his enthusiasm. The score is already sold to an English publisher. It will appear in Italian. And now you have all my news; send me yours.

The Grand Duke of Weimar has written to me, through his private secretary, to congratulate me on the success of the *Troyens*. His letter has appeared everywhere. Is it not a charming piece of attention? There is no one more gracious, no one more princely, no such intelligent Mæcenas. He is just what you would have been, had you been a prince.

CVIII.

DECEMBER 14, 1863.

Thanks, my dear friend, for your anxiety. I am still subject to fits of coughing which produce spasms and sickness, but I go out all the same, and I have been present at the last three performances of our opera. I have not written to you for the simple reason that I had too many things to say to you. I am not sending you the newspapers; my son is amusing himself by collecting all the eulogistic or favourable notices, of which there are now sixty-four. I had a charming letter yesterday from a lady, a Greek I imagine, the Countess Callimachi; I cried over it.

The performance last night was superb; Madames Charton and Monjanze are really improving every day. How unfortunate it is that we have only five more performances! Madame Charton leaves us at the end of the month; she made a considerable sacrifice in accepting the engagement for the *Troyens* at the Théâtre-Lyrique, notwithstanding that she receives six thousand francs a month. There is not another Dido in France; there is nothing for it but resignation, but the work is known, and that is the important point.

The scene between Chorœbus and Cassandra in the first act, the *Prise de la Troie*, is to be performed at a Court concert at Weimar on the 1st of January.

I am writing like a cat; I am thoroughly worn out. Sleep is overcoming me ; it is noon.

CIX.

JANUARY 8, 1864.

My Dear Humbert,

I have been confined to my bed again for the last nine days, and am taking advantage of a moment when I am comparatively free from suffering to write and thank you for your letter. I would also send you your four-part hymn if I had the score of *Alceste*, but I must obtain the loan of a copy. Your lines very nearly fit the music, but there are a few sylla-bles too many, and they have compelled you to alter the divine melody. I fear also that in order to render the air, which should not be forced, easier to sing, you will be obliged to lower it a minor third (in G natural), especially if you have soprano voices, without which half the effect would be lost.

My son left the day before yesterday. The

fictitious poem which you mention was written by a gentleman who has been one of my energetic supporters, but, unfortunately, his poetry is so bad that he ought to be careful not to show it to anybody. I have no strength to write more; my head is like a hollow old nut.

Thank Madame Ferrand for her kind message.

CX.

JANUARY 12, 1864.

MY DEAR HUMBERT,

Do not be so impatient. I have not yet been able to get hold of a copy of the full score of *Alceste*. The other day I had the pianoforte arrangement sent to me, but the arranger (the wretch!) has taken the liberty of altering the progression. However, you shall have your chant in a few days.

I must tell you once more that your lines do not go exactly with the music. You must not let French prejudices weigh with you to the extent of adapting perfect lines to this sublime music; the first line should consist of nine feet with a feminine termination; the second, of ten feet with a masculine termination; the third like the first, and the fourth like the second.

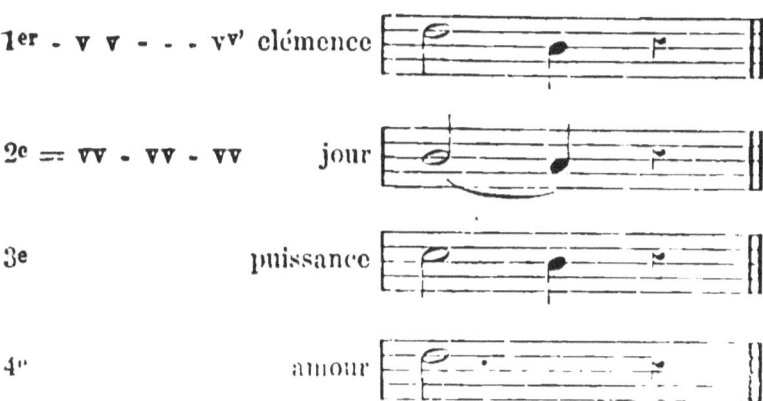

But I will point all this out more clearly when I send you the manuscript. The words should fit the music, so perfectly beautiful, like a drapery sculptured by Phidias on a nude statue. Seek it patiently, and you will find it. Words have been put to the same chant in England for use in the Protestant churches; I would rather not know them.

The gentleman you mentioned to me the other day has sent me some more verses this morning. I enclose them.

I am still in bed.

CXI.

THURSDAY MORNING, JANUARY 12, 1864.

MY DEAR FRIEND,

I had already seen the article in the *Contemporain*; the author sent me a copy together with a very kind letter.

Gaspérini intends shortly to hold a public con-
ference on the *Troyens*.

I have just corrected the first proof of your
hymn. You will receive your copies in a few
days.

Good-bye. I am in such terrible pain this
morning that writing is a horrible exertion.

CXII.

JANUARY 17, 1864.

MY DEAR FRIEND,

You have hit upon the very thing. It
is ineffably sublime, and enough to make the
very stones of the temple weep. There is no
need of a second couplet, as each repetition
should be sang twice. It would be too long,
and the effect would be marred considerably.
You will notice two or three alterations of
syllables, which you can arrange as you think
best. As the parts are not all paralled, it was
necessary, in the case of the tenors and basses,
to make these alterations. I must tell you that,
in certain passages, the counter-tenor part is
very badly written by Glück; no pupil ever dare
show his master a lesson in harmony so clumsily
arranged in some respects. But the bass, the
harmony, and the melody make the whole composition sublime. If you are going to depend

upon women and children I think you might
leave the chant in G, but they must not scream;
it should be breathed forth like a sigh of celestial love. If not, transpose it into E sharp.

CXIII.

APRIL 12, 1864.

MY DEAR HUMBERT,

Thanks for your letter, and for the
somewhat satisfactory news you give me about
your health. I verily believe the sun is at
length showing some inclination to smile upon
us. We both of us stand in urgent need of
warmth. I am almost as sorely tried as you are
by my infernal neuralgia. I spend eighteen
hours out of the twenty-four in bed. I do
nothing but suffer. I have resigned my post on
the *Débats*. I agree with you that you ought to
have your hymn to Glück's music stereotyped; but select the best stereotypist in Lyon,
and when your proofs have been corrected re-
vise them yourself, word for word and note for
note. It will not cost much; and if the churches
take it up it may bring you in some money. It
is to your interest not to put a higher price
upon it than two francs a copy. The expenses
should not amount to more than thirty francs,
all told.

Good-bye. I have come to the end of my strength, and I must close my letter.

CXIV.

PARIS, MAY 4, 1864.

How are you, my dear friend, by night and by day? I am taking advantage of a few hours' respite granted me by my pains to ask after yours.

It is cold and raining; some prosaic sadness or other is hovering in the air. One portion of our little musical world, the one I belong to, is melancholy; the other is gay, because Meyerbeer is dead. We were to have dined together last week, but he failed to keep the appointment.

Let me hear if you have come across a composition called *Tristia*, with this motto from Ovid,

Qui viderit illas
De lacrymis factas sentiet esse meis.

If you have not it I will send it to you, because you like to read lively things. I have never heard the work. I think the first chorus in prose, *Ce monde entier n'est qu'une ombre fugitive*, is worth hearing. I composed it in Rome in 1831.

If we could only have a chat together, and I could be quite close to your arm-chair, I think I could make you forget your sufferings. The voice and the eye have a certain power which is not possessed by paper. Have you flowers and and newly bursting foliage outside your windows? I have nothing but stone walls outside mine. Out in the street a cur has been howling for the last hour, a parrot is screaming, and a paraquet is imitating the twittering of the sparrows; in a court-yard some washerwomen are singing, and another parrot is shrieking incessantly *Portez ... arms!* What can one do? The day is very long. My son is on board his ship again, and will sail from Saint Nazaire for Mexico a week hence. He was reading some of your letters the other day, and he congratulated me upon being your friend. He is a good lad, and his heart and mind have developed richly, though tardily. Fortunately for me I have some musical neighbours close at hand, who are very kind to me. I go to their house frequently in the evening, and I am allowed to lie full length on the sofa and listen to the conversation without being expected to take any great part in it. No fools ever intrude there, but in the event of such a catastrophe happening it is understood that I may go away without a word. I have not had an attack of musical fever for a long time, but Th. Ritter is giving Beethoven's five *concertos* with a delicious orchestra at his fortnightly concerts, and I go and listen to those marvels. Our *Harold* has just been performed for the second time in New York with great success. What have these Americans got into their heads?

Good-bye. Do not tire yourself by writing more than half a dozen lines.

CXV.

PARIS, AUGUST 18, 1864.

MY DEAR HUMBERT,

I have not left Paris, my son having come to spend a fortnight with me. I was absolutely alone, my mother-in-law being at Luxeuil, and my friends scattered abroad—some in Switzerland, some in Italy, &c., &c.

I was going to write to you when your letter arrived. The value of the cross of an *Officier** is enhanced by the charming letter in which, contrary to custom, Marshall Vaillant announced the honour. Two days later there was

---

* Berlioz was made an *Officier* of the Legion of Honour on the 12th of August, 1864.

a grand banquet at the Ministry, where all the official world, and the Minister in particular, overwhelmed me with attention. They all seemed to be saying, " Pray forgive us for having forgotten you." As a matter of fact, twenty-nine years have elapsed since I was gazetted *Chevalier*. Mérimee, too, said, as he shook me by the hand, " This proves that I have never been a minister."

Congratulations are showered upon me because everybody knows that I have never asked for anything of the kind. But it is a miracle to find any thought bestowed upon a savage who never asks for anything.

I am invariably ill one day out of every two. However, for the last few days I do not seem to have suffered so acutely. Yes, there has been some talk lately of reproducing the *Troyens*, but it is anything but pleasing to me, and I have written to Madame Charton-Demeur, warning her not to accept any offer that may be made to her. The Théâtre-Lyrique is simply impossible, and its Director, who always poses as a collaborator, is more impossible still.

You do not tell me how you treat your neuralgia. Do you suffer reasonably or unreasonably? Have you any luxury in your pain, or merely what is absolutely necessary? My poor friend, we may both of us well say of each other, *Misero succurrere disco.*

Louis will be off again in a few hours, and I shall fall back into a state of complete isolation. I have a wretched headache. Remember me to Madame Ferrand and your brother.

P.S.—A stroke of Providence, easily foreseen; Scudo, my bitter enemy on the *Revue des Deux Mondes*, has gone mad.

CXVI.

PARIS, OCTOBER 28, 1864.

MY DEAR HUMBERT,

On my return from a trip to Dauphiné I found your letter, which has saddened me. You had as much as you could do to write at all, and yet your young friend, M. Bernard, told me that you go out frequently with the aid of a friendly arm. I do not know what to think. Have you become worse recently? As far as I am concerned I derived considerable benefit from my stay in the country with my nieces; but now my neuralgic pains have taken possession of me, and torment me regularly from eight o'clock in the morning until three in the after-

noon, in addition to which I am suffering from
an obstinate sore throat, to say nothing of
weariness and vexation. I could write you
quires about it all. However, on the other
hand, there are some satisfactory realities; my
son is now a captain, and is in command of the
good ship *La Louisiane*, at this time on her
voyage to Mexico. The poor boy had hard
work to resign himself to the prospect of only
seeing me for a few days every four or five
months; our affection for each other is inexpressible.

The musical world of Paris has reached a
pitch of corruption beyond conception. I am
becoming more and more isolated every day.
Béatrice et Bénédict is in preparation at Stutt-
gard now. I shall, perhaps, go and conduct the
first performance. I have also had an offer for
St. Petersburg in March, but I shall not accept
unless the terms are sufficiently favourable to
compensate me for braving the terrible Russian
climate once more. If I go it will be for Louis'
sake; as far as I am concerned a few thousand
francs, more or less, will not alter my existence
to any appreciable extent. Perhaps the trips
I should so much like to take would be easier
for me; there is one especially, *which you wot of,*

that I would undertake often, for it seems very
hard that I cannot see you. I was several times
on the point of setting out to pay you a visit at
Couzieux during the time I was in the country,
not far from Vienna, but business called me to
Grenoble; and, moreover, as the time for the
reopening of the Conservatoire was at hand, and
I had not asked for leave of absence, I was
bound to return to Paris. Auguste Berlioz,
whom I met at Grenoble, will have told you all
about me.

I do not quite know how to account for the
flatteries which are now heaped upon me by so
many people. I have enough compliments paid
me to turn any ordinary head, and I invariably
feel a desire to say to my toadies, " But, sir (or
madame), you forget that I am a critic no
longer, and that I have given up writing
articles."

The monotony of my existence was enlivened
to a certain extent three days ago, when
Madame Erard, Madame Spontini, and their
niece asked me to read Shakespeare's *Othello* to
them some morning when I could find time for it.
We arranged a meeting, and put "no ad-
mittance" upon the door of the Chateau de la
Muette, where these ladies live. Orders were

given to refuse ingress to all bores and idiots who might disturb us, and I read the masterpiece from one end to the other, giving myself full play just as if I had been alone. I had only six persons to listen to me, and they all wept splendidly.

My God, what a stupendous revelation of the depths of the human heart ! What a sublime angel is Desdemona! And what a noble, though unhappy man is Othello ! What a frightful demon Iago is ! And to think that a being of our species wrote it all !

How we two should electrify each other could we but read these sublimities together occasionally ! Much and careful study is needed to look at such a work from the author's point of view, to understand him thoroughly, and to follow the lofty flights of his genius. And translators are such asses ! In my copy I have corrected I do not know how many blunders made by M. Benjamin Laroche, and yet he is more faithful and less ignorant than any of the others.

Liszt has been spending a week in Paris; we dined together twice, and as musical conversation was prudently interdicted, we passed some charming hours. He has left for Rome, where he is playing the *music of the future* to the Pope, who wants to know what it means.

The success of *Roland à Roncevaux* at the Opéra surpasses, so far as receipts are concerned, all previous experiences. It is the work of an inferior amateur, and incredibly flat; the author is supremely ignorant, and is astounded at his good luck. But the story is admirable and he has been clever enough to turn it to advantage. The Emperor went to hear it twice in one week: he summoned the author* to his box, he has given the cue to the critics, and the world of chauvinism has dubbed him Charlemagne. Pshaw!

Commedianti! Shakespeare was right. " All the world's a stage." How lucky I am in not being obliged to give an account of the occurrence!

You know that our worthy Scudo, my insulter on the *Revue des Deux Mondes*, is dead. He died a raving maniac. In my opinion, his madness was evident more than fifteen years ago. Death has some good in it, much good; one must not abuse it.

Good-bye, my dear, my very dear friend. Seeing that we still live, do not let us remain

* M. Mermet, son of a General of the First Empire.

alive without telling each other how we are getting on.

CXVII.

Paris, November 10, 1864.

My Dear Humbert,

As it seems that my letters are a source of pleasure to you, I do not see why I should deny myself the happiness of writing to you. What can I do better? Positively nothing. I always feel less unhappy after having chatted with you, or heard from you. I have an ever increasing admiration for our civilization, with its posts, its telegraphs, its steam, its electricity, those slaves to human will, which allow thought to be transmitted with such rapidity.

Some means should also be discovered for preventing thought from being so sad as a rule. The only one we know of at present is to be young, beloved, free, and a lover of the beauties of nature and mighty art. You and I are neither young, nor beloved, nor free, nor even in good health, so we must needs content ourselves and rejoice over what is left to us. Hippocrates said, *ars longa;* we should say, *ars æterna,* and we should prostrate ourselves before its eternity.

True it is that this adoration of art renders us cruelly exacting, and makes every-day life, which alas! is the real life, press twice as heavily upon us. What are we to do? To hope? To despair? To resign ourselves? To sleep? To die? Not so. After all, by faith alone we are saved; by faith only we are lost. "All the world's a stage." What world? The earth? The world of fashion? And are there players, too, in the other worlds? Are the dramas there as sad or as visible as among us? Are their theatres as tardy in enlighten-ment, and have their audiences time to grow old before their eyes are opened so that they see clearly?

The pitching and rolling of the heart, in-evitable ideas! A wretched ship which knows that even the compass gets out of order during a storm! *Sunt lacrymæ rerum.*

Would you believe, my dear Humbert, that I cannot make up my mind about the past? I cannot understand why I did not know Virgil; it seems to me that I see him; mild, affable, and accessable, dreaming in his Sicilian villa. And Shakespeare, that mighty indifferent man, impassable as a mirror. And yet he must

have been endowed with an immense, universal
pity. And Beethoven, contemptuous and uncouth, yet gifted with such profund sensibility.
It seems to me that I should have forgiven him
everything, contempt, brutality, and all. And
Glück the superb !

Send me the march out of *Alceste* with your
words; I will find means of having it stereotyped without any expense to you. You will
not get paid for your poetry, but you will be
none the less abused for having composed it.

Last week, M. Blanche, the doctor of the
lunatic asylum at Passy, invited a goodly array
of *savants* and artists to celebrate the anniversary of the first performance of the *Troyens*. I
was invited without having the slightest sus-
picion of what was in contemplation. Gounod,
Doli fabricator Epeus, was there; and with his
weak voice, but deep feeling, sang the duet,
O nuit d'ivresse. Madame Barthe Bauderali sang
the music of Dido, and then Gounod gave us
the song of Hylos, unaccompanied. A young
lady sang the dance music, and I was made to
recite, without music, Dido's scene, *Va, ma sœur*,
l'implorer. I assure you, the Virgillian passage
produced an immense effect—

Terque quaterque manu pectus percussa decorum
Flarentesque abscissa comas.

Everybody knew the score almost by heart. We missed you.

CXVIII.

DECEMBER 12, 1864,

MY DEAR FERRAND,

I was beginning to be rather anxious about you; it is nothing but a question of a fresh access of pain. I am going to have your hymn stereotyped. There may, possibly, be some delay, as the journeymen stereotypers and printers are on strike, and we shall have to wait until the crisis is at an end. I have arranged the words to a certain extent wherever you have left them blank, but you will have to make a few alterations. The first, for instance, is impossible ; the mute syllable *je* is horrible on such a long note. It would completely spoil the very commencement.

The first line of the second couplet, on the contrary, goes very well. You should take it as your model. Another invocation, *O*, would do wonders. And do your best to get rid of *en ce jour* and *dès ce jour* in the same couplet.

There is also an error of prosody in the following phrase, which appears twice,

Inef—fable ivresse.

It would be better to transpose it thus:

Ivres—se ineffable.

But that would destroy the line. Look over it again; the sentiment of your words is so beautiful that they ought to be allied to the music in a manner beyond reproach.

I have just received a telegram from the director of the Academy of Singing at Vienna, informing me that yesterday, in honour of my birthday, the double chorus from the *Damnation de Faust* was performed at a concert given by the Society. *Villes entourées de murs et ramparts. Jam nox stellata velamina pandit.* The chorus was encored amid immense applause.

Is not that a charmingly cordial piece of German attention?

Good-bye; send me your corrections as soon as you have gone over them carefully. The work must be without a flaw, like a diamond.

P.S.—You cannot say *ve-*nez (nor *de ne*) *pouvoir*; it is detestable.

Why do you not put your name on the title-page? It ought to appear there.

I think it will be necessary to transpose the piece into F; certain bars are too high for the *soprani* and the tenors, and it ought to be sung without the least effort.

What has Jouvin been doing to you? Has
he written you any fresh insults? He is a re-
lation of M. Gauthier's, of Grenoble, and is on
the staff of the *Figaro.*

Louis has not returned from Mexico yet. He
wrote to me from Martinique. He sailed his
ship successfully through a storm which lasted
for four days, and knocked everybody up.
When he arrived at the Antilles he was congratulated by the authorities, and received his
definite commission as captain.

Good-bye to you and yours. If writing
over-fatigues you, ask your brother to write for
you.

CXIX.

PARIS, DECEMBER 23, 1864.

MY DEAR FRIEND,

Your words are perfect, and the whole
thing goes well. I have spoken to Brandus
who is perfectly willing to print the hymn and
give you twenty copies. His printer has not
joined the strike, so that your little publication
will be put in hand at once. My copyist is
transposing it into F, and I will put the words
to his copy to-morrow, after which I will urge
the printer to hurry on with it. Brandus will be
able to make the work known and push the sale

of it through the *Gazette Musicale*. The title-page shall be as you wish.

I am sending you a number of the *Nation*, in which Gaspérini has written two columns on the *Troyens*' affair at the *Conservatoire*.

Glück's letter was new to me. Where the deuce did you pick it up? The same thing happened everywhere and always. Beethoven was insulted to a greater extent even than Glück. Weber and Spontini were similarly honoured. M. de Flotow, the composer of *Marta*, met with nothing but praise. This dull opera is performed in every language and in every theatre in the world. I went the other day to hear the charming little Patti, who played Marta; when I came out I seemed to be covered from head to foot with fleas, just as if I had been in a pigeon-house, and I sent word to that marvellous child that though I freely forgave her for making me listen to such platitudes, I could never do it again.

Fortunately, it contains the delicious Irish melody *The Last Rose of Summer*, which she sings with an amount of poetical simplicity whose sweet perfume almost succeeds in disinfecting the remainder of the score.

I will send Louis your congratulations; he

will be very grateful for them, as he has read
your letters, and has congratulated me on having
such a friend as you.

CXX.

JANUARY 25, 1865.

MY DEAR HUMBERT,

The final proof of your hymn has just
reached me. It is at last free from blunders.
It is to be printed at once, and you will receive
your copies very soon.

Last Sunday our overture to the *Francs
Juges*, played at the Cirque Napoleon by the
large orchestra of the Popular Concerts, to an
audience of four thousand, produced a gigantic
effect. The *couple* who hiss me as a rule did
not fail to put in an appearance, and they made
themselves heard after the third round of applause, the result being three more rounds and
an enthusiastic encore. When I came out I was
waylaid on the Boulevards, ladies asked to be
introduced to me, and unknown youths stepped
forward to shake hands with me. It was a
curious sight. And to think that it was you,
my dear friend, who, *thirty seven years ago*, made
me write this overture, my first attempt at instrumental music.

I have just received an American newspaper containing a very flattering article upon the performance, in New York, of the *Roi Lear* overture, the sister one to that of the *Francs Juges*. What a pity it is that one cannot live a hundred and fifty years! What a splendid revenge one would have on this race of idiots!

How are you getting on, my dear friend, in this infamous season of fog, snow, rain, mud, wind, cold and chilblains?

Our friends and acquaintances are fading away like the grass. We have no less than three dying members in our section at the Institut. My friend Wallace is dying; Felicien David is in the same state; Scudo is dead, and so is that worthy old ass, Proudhon. What is going to become of us? Happily, Azevedo, Jouvin, and Scholl remain behind.

CXXI.

FEBRUARY 8, 1865.

MY DEAR FRIEND,

Twenty-four copies of your hymn were sent to you a week ago; you must have received them by this time.

I am getting up; it is six o'clock in the afternoon; I took some drops of laudanum yesterday, and was completely stupified. What a life ! And yet I would lay a wager you are still worse.

Nevertheless, I shall go out this evening to hear Beethoven's septet. I am looking forward to being warmed by that masterpiece. My favourite *virtuosi* are to play it.

The day after to-morrow I am to read *Hamlet* at Massart's house to an audience of five. Shall I have strength enough? It will last five hours. There is only one among the five, Madame Massart, who has even a vague idea of the great work. The rest, who have begged and prayed me to give the reading, know literally nothing about it.

I am almost afraid of seeing artistic natures suddenly brought face to face with this grand phenomenon of genius. I can only liken them to persons born blind and suddenly endowed with the sense of sight. I know them and I think they will understand. But imagine anybody having lived forty-five or fifty years without knowing *Hamlet!* One might as well spend one's life in a coal mine. Shakespeare said, "Glory is like a circle on the water, which goes on enlarging until it disappears altogether."

Good-morning, my dear friend. The post is

good enough to take charge of this letter; I have no doubt it will display an equal amount of amiability in bringing me one from you very shortly.

CXXII.

APRIL 26, 1865.

MY DEAR FRIEND,

Forgive me for having caused you anxiety by my silence; I am so weakened and stupified by my sufferings that, having recently written a letter to my son in which I spoke much *of* you, I imagined I had spoken *to* you. I really thought I had written to you. I have executed your commission in connection with de Carné, and I personally handed to him the diploma intended for him, but tell me if anybody, and if so who, is to be thanked for this nomination to the Institut d'Egypt, for I am entirely ignorant on the subject.

I took a trip three weeks ago to Saint-Nazaire to see my son, who had arrived from Mexico and was on the point of sailing thither again. I spent three days in bed there. My dear Louis is in a good position now; he is an officer of the mercantile marine before whom his inferiors tremble, and for whom his superiors have nothing but warm praise. Our mutual affection does nothing but increase.

Your brother has, apparently, been a source of severe disappointment to you; I hope that the affair, of which I know nothing, has become less troublesome by this time.

How can I tell you what is brewing in this musical eating-house, Paris! I have left it, and shall never enter it again. I have been to a general rehearsal of Meyerbeer's *Africaine*, which lasted from half-past seven to half-past one. I thought I should never come back any more.

The famous German violinist, Joachim, is here on a visit for ten days; he plays every evening somewhere or other. I have heard Beethoven's pianoforte trio in B flat, the *sonata* in A, and the quartet in E minor, played by him and other first-rate artistes—the music of the starry spheres. You may well imagine—more than that, you understand how impossible it is, after having become acquainted with such miracles of inspiration, to endure ordinary music, patented productions, and works recommended by the Mayor or the Minister of Public Instruction.

If I am able to undertake a trip away from Paris this summer, I shall give you a call and shake hands with you. I must go to Geneva, Vienne, and Grenoble, all very far distant from Couzieux. I will do my utmost, you may be sure. We are both of us alive still, a somewhat extraordinary coincidence, and we ought to take advantage of it.

CXXIII.

MAY 8, 1865.

MY DEAR HUMBERT,

I have seen M. Vervoite, who told me precisely what I expected to hear. The Society which he directs makes its money entirely through the good offices of four hundred lady patronesses who dispose of tickets *when they take an interest in the bénificiaire.* A provincial institution of which they know nothing would be a matter of indifference to them ; not a penny would be made, and you would have to guarantee eight hundred francs for expenses. It is, therefore, no use dreaming of it.

I am going to write, trusting somewhat to chance, to the Secretary of the Institut d'Egypt, whose name is, as usual, illegible. As for my *Traité d'instrumentation,* it could not possibly be of any use in connection with the reorganization of the Sultan's military bands. The work

is intended to teach composers how to employ
the various instruments to the best advantage,
not to teach performers how to play those same
instruments. You might just as well send a
score or any other book whatever. Moreover,
my sending it would look like asking for a
donation.

I fully sympathise, my very dear friend, with
you in your brother's misfortune, but I have
not courage enough to offer you idle consolation.

My son should be in Mexico by this time; he
will be greatly pleased, on his return, by your
kind messages for him. Good-bye, I am so ill
that I can scarcely write.

CXXIV.

DECEMBER 23, 1865.

My DEAR HUMBERT,

I am merely writing a line to thank
you for your cordial letter. The echo which
answers me from the depths of your soul would
make me very happy if I could ever be so again;
but I am past everything but suffering of all
kinds. I have been wanting to answer you for
several days past, but I have not been able : I
have been in too great pain. I have spent five

days in bed, incapable of an idea, and vainly summoning sleep to my aid. I am rather better to-day. I have just got up, and am writing to you before going to our meeting at the Institut. Good morning, and thank you for your friendship, your indulgence, and everything that makes you so intelligent, so sensible, and so good.

In truth, I can write no more.

CXXV.

JANUARY 17, 1866.

MY DEAR HUMBERT,

I am writing to you this evening, alone by my fireside. Louis sent me word this morning of his arrival in France, and mentioned you. He has read several of your letters, and appreciates your deep friendship for his father. I have, moreover, been violently agitated this morning. *Armide* is in course of reproduction at the Théâtre-Lyrique, and the Director has asked me to superintend the study of it, so ill-adapted to this world of shop-keepers.

Madame Charton-Demeur, who plays the trying part of Armide, comes every day to rehearse with M. Saint-Saëns, a great pianist, and a great musician who knows his Glück almost as well as I do. It is very curious to see this poor lady groping about in the sublime, and to witness the gradual enlightenment of her intelligence. This morning Saint-Saëns and I shook hands over one act. We were choking. Never did any other man discover such *accents*. And to think that there are people who blaspheme this masterpiece, admiring it meanwhile, and that it is attacked, bespattered with mud, cut in pieces, reviled, and insulted everywhere by great and small, singers, directors, *conductors*, publishers, everybody—

> *Oh! les misérables!*
> *O ciel! quelle horrible menace!*
> *Je frémis, tout mon sang se glace!*
> *Amour, puissant amour, viens calmer mon effroi,*
> *Et prends pitié d'un cœur qui s'abandonne à toi.*

This belongs to another world! Would that I could see you there! Would you believe that since I have plunged into music once more, my pains have gradually disappeared? I get up every day now, just as everybody else does. But I shall have some cruel sufferings to undergo at the hands of these actors, and especially the conductor of the orchestra. That will happen in April.

Madame Fournier wrote to me the other day to tell me that a gentleman whom she met at Geneva had spoken to her in terms of warm praise about our *Troyens*. So much the better. But it would have been better for me if I had written some villainy after the manner of Offenbach. What will these Parisian frogs say about *Armide?*

Why have I written this? It is a confidence which I could not restrain. Forgive me.

CXXVI.

MARCH 8, 1866.

My DEAR HUMBERT,

I am writing to you this morning for the express purpose of telling you what happened yesterday at an "extraordinary grand" concert, given under the direction of Pasdeloup in the Cirque Napoleon at three times the usual prices of admission, in aid of a charitable society.

The septet out of the *Troyens* was performed for the first time, with Madame Charton, a hundred and fifty chorus singers, and the usual large and fine orchestra. The whole of the programme was very badly received by the audience, with the exception of the march out of Wagner's *Lohengrin*. Meyerbeer's overture to the *Prophète* was hissed to such an extent that the police had to interfere and turn out the offenders.

Last of all came the septet. Immense applause and cries of *bis*. An even better performance the second time. I was seen perched on my bench, for which I had to pay three francs (they had not sent me a single ticket), the applause began over again, hats and handkerchiefs were waved, and there was a shout of "Long live Berlioz! Get up, we want to see you!" I did my best to hide myself, but I was surrounded when I got out on to the Boulevard. This morning I have received numerous visits, and a charming letter from Legouvé's daughter.

Liszt was there; I saw him from my lofty perch; he had just arrived from Rome, and knew nothing about the *Troyens*. Why were you not there? There were at least three thousand people present. Formerly this would have rejoiced me greatly.

The effect was very grand, especially the passage with the noise of the sea, which cannot be rendered on the piano—

Et la mer endormie
Murmine en sommeillant les accords les plus doux.

I was profoundly moved by it. My neighbours in the pit, who did not know me, as soon as they learnt that I was the author of the piece, shook me by the hand and thanked me in all sorts of curious ways. Why were not you there? It is sad, but it is beautiful!

Regina gravi jamdudun saucia curâ.

Written after having rehearsed *Armide* ten times with Madame Charton.

CXXVII.

MARCH 9, 1866.

MY DEAR FRIEND,

I am adding a few lines to my letter of yesterday. A small amateur Society has just written me a collective note, bearing their various signatures, upon the success of the day before yesterday. This letter is, strange to say, a somewhat modified copy of the one I wrote to Spontini twenty-two years ago, on the occasion of the performance of *Fernan Cortez*. You will find it in my volume, *Soirées de l'Orchestre*. The only difference consists in their having put, " The *septet from the Troyens* was performed yesterday at the Cirque," in place of what I said to Spontini.

Is it not a charming idea to apply to me, after

a lapse of twenty-two years, what I myself wrote to Spontini? It has touched me, I assure you.

P.S.—You will find my letter to Spontini at page 185 of the *Soirées*.

CXXVIII.

MARCH 16, 1866.

MY DEAR HUMBERT,

The *Soirées de l'Orchestre*, which I felt sure I had given you, will be sent to you to-day. Let me know whether you have the other two volumes, *Grotesques de la Musique* and *A Travers Chants*.

The performance of the septet is creating more and more sensation. Liszt's *Mass* was given at Saint-Eustache yesterday. There was an immense crowd, but, alas! what a denial of art!

I am not in bed as you are, but I am none the better for being up.

CXXIX.

MARCH 22, 1866.

MY DEAR HUMBERT,

I am very glad that the volume of the *Soirées* did not, as the *Mémoires* did, take a fortnight to reach to. I am going to send you *Grotesques de la Musique* and *A Travers Chants.* I cannot write anything on them because, if I do, the post-office will refuse to take them.

Neither the revolution scene out of *Cortes,* nor the chorus from the *Danaïdes,* is published separately, and in regard to the septet, let me beg of you not to let your young people attempt to sing it. They would make a fearful mess of it, a regular *charivari,* to a certainty. Besides, you could no more do without the chorus than the chorus could do without the septet.

Three fragments of the *Fuite en Egypte* are to be played at the Conservatoire on Easter Sunday. In the meantime that silly Pasdeloup is announcing for Sunday next the *overture* to the *Fuite en Egypte,* that is to say, the miniature symphony during which the Shepherds are supposed to arrive close to the stable at Bethlehem. I have just written to ask him to do nothing of the sort, but I will lay a wager he will be obstinate. It is absurd, because this movement cannot be taken apart from the chorus which follows.

I have seen du Boys; he is a candidate for the seat in the Academy of Moral Sciences at the Institut, vacant by the death of M.

Béranger. Yesterday we buried our *confrère*,. Clapisson. It is thought that Gounod will succeed him.

The length of your letter leads me to hope that you are somewhat better.

CXXX.

NOVEMBER 10, 1866.

MY DEAR HUMBERT,

I ought to be at Vienna, but I was informed by telegram the other day that the concert had been unavoidably postponed until the 16th of December; I shall, therefore, not start until the 5th of next month. I suppose the *Damnation de Faust* is not sufficiently studied to please them, and they do not want to let me hear it only half known. I shall really enjoy going to hear it, seeing that I have not listened to it from beginning to end since Dresden, a dozen years ago.

Your note reached me this morning while I was in the midst of one of my paroxysms of pain which nothing can charm away. I am writing in bed between the intervals of rubbing myself. Nevertheless, I thank you ; your letters always do me so much good that at any other moment the remedy would have been effectual.

The rehearsals of *Alceste* have reanimated me to a certain extent. Never has the masterpiece appeared to me so grandly beautiful, and, undoubtedly, never has Glück been so worthily performed. An entire generation is now hearing this marvel for the first time, and is prostrating itself in love before the inspiration of the *maestro*. The other day there was a lady sitting close to me who shed such noisy tears that she attracted the attention of everybody. I have received a shoal of letters thanking me for the care I bestowed upon Glück's work. Perrin is now anxious to put *Armide* on the stage again. Ingres is by no means the only one among our *confrères* at the Institut who habitually attends the performances of *Alceste;* the majority of the painters and sculptors are gifted with a love for the antique, a love of the beautiful which no amount of suffering can transform.

The Queen of Thessaly is a second Niobe, and, nevertheless, in her concluding air in the second act,

Ah! malgré moi mon faible cœur partage,

the expression is carried to such a pitch as to make one almost dizzy.

I am going to send you the small score; you

will be able to read it easily, and it will enable you to spend a few pleasant moments.

Good-bye; I can do no more.

CXXXI.

DECEMBER 30, 1866.

MY DEAR FRIEND,

Here I am, back again from Vienna, and writing half a dozen lines to tell you so. I do not know if the *Union* has reported the tremendous success of the *Damnation de Faust* in Austria. In any case, I may as well tell you that it was the greatest success I ever achieved in my life. There were four hundred performers, and three thousand listeners in that immense Salle des Redoutes. The enthusiasm surpassed all my previous experiences of that kind of thing. On the following day, my room was filled with flowers, garlands, visitors, and embracers. In the evening there was a *fête* in my honour, with no end of speeches in French and German. The one made by Prince Czartoriski made an especial sensation. I was, nevertheless, very ill, but I had a splendid leader of the orchestra, who conducted some of the rehearsals when I was too exhausted to do so.

I send you a cutting from a French newspaper.

Good-bye; I should be very happy for a quarter of an hour if I only knew that you were in better health and spirits. I embrace you with all my heart.

CXXXII.

PARIS, JANUARY 11, 1867.

MY DEAR FRIEND,

It is midnight. I am writing to you from my bed, as I always do, and my letter will find you in yours, as usual. Your last note distressed me; its curtness revealed your suffering. I wanted to reply to you forthwith, but intolerable pain, sleeping for twenty hours at a stretch, medical nonsense, friction under chloroform, doses of laudanum which were futile and only productive of fatiguing dreams, prevented me. I can see very clearly now that we shall have hard work to shake hands. You cannot stir, and the slightest change of quarters, at all events for three-quarters and a half of the year, kills me. I have no idea what the country is like at Couzieux, or of your *home*, as the English say, your existence, or your surroundings. I do

not *see* you as you are, and this fact redoubles
my sadness on your account. What is to be
done? The journey from Vienna has all but
put an end to me, and neither the success, the
pleasure of so much applause, or the wonderful
performance, can compensate me. The cold of
our frightful climate is fatal to me. My dear
Louis wrote to me the day before yesterday, de-
scribing his morning rides in the forests of
Martinique, the tropical vegetation, and the sun,
the real sun. I am inclined to think that it is
the very thing we both need, you and I. Of what
use is mighty nature if we die far away from
her and in ignorance of her sublime beauties?
My dear friend!—The stupid rumbling of carriages disturbs the silence of the night—Paris,
damp, cold, and muddy! Parisian Paris!—now
everything is quiet—sleeping the sleep of the
unjust—well, sleeplessness *sans phrases*, as one
of the brigands of the first revolution said.

I will send you *Alceste* as soon as I can stir
out. I do not understand your question about
the small score of the *Damnation de Faust*.
What do you mean when you ask me *if there is
another besides the first?* What first? The title
is *Légende dramatique* in four acts? Have you
it? Let me know also whether you have the

large score of my *Messe des Morts*. If I were threatened with the destruction of the whole of my works save one, I would crave mercy for the *Messe des Morts*. A new edition is being prepared in Milan now; if you have not it, I could, I imagine, send it you six or seven weeks hence.

Do not forget any of my questions, and answer them as soon as you are strong enough. Alas! it is not leisure which fails you.

Good-bye, my dear friend. I am going to lie awake and think of you, for *non suadent cadentia sidera somnos*.

CXXXIII.

PARIS, FEBRUARY 2, 1867.

MY DEAR HUMBERT,

You have written me two charming pages; half a page would have sufficed to let me know that you had received the two scores. You are far more courageous than I am. So much the better! It proves to me that you are not so ill as I am; at least, I am vain enough to think so. I still suffer very much. I want to write to you, but I cannot.

Good-bye. At all events, I have said "good morning" to you.

CXXXIV.

JUNE 11, 1867.

MY DEAR FRIEND,

Thank you for your letter, which has done me much good. Yes, I am in Paris, but still so unwell that at this moment I have scarcely strength enough to write to you. I am ill in every way; I am tormented by anxiety. Louis is still on the shores of Mexico, and I have not heard from him for a long time. I dread those Mexican brigands.

The Exhibition has made Paris like the infernal regions. I have not been to it yet. I walk with difficulty, and it is not easy to get a carriage now. There was a grand *fête* at Court yesterday. I was invited, but when the time came for me to go I had not strength enough to dress myself.

I see very clearly that you are not a bit more valiant than I am, and I thank you a thousand times for your goodness in letting me hear from you now and then.

I was writing these few lines to you from the Conservatoire, when the jury, of whom I am one, for the competition in musical composition at the Exhibition had to assemble. I was interrupted by a summons to the meeting, and to award the prize. On the preceding days we heard a hundred and four *cantatas*, and J had the pleasure of witnessing the coronation (unanimous) of my young friend Camille Saint-Saëns, one of the greatest musicians of the present day.

You have evidently not read the numerous newspapers which have spoken about my *Roméo et Juliette* in connection with Gounod's opera, and after a fashion not at all agreeable for him. It is a success in which I have had no hand, and which has astonished me more than a little.

I was urgently requested a few days ago by some Americans to go to New York, where, as they say, I am popular. Last year our symphony, *Harold en Italie*, was performed there five times with ever-increasing success, and an amount of applause worthy of Vienna.

I am altogether upset by this meeting of the jury. How happy Saint-Saëns will be! I went straight to his house to tell him of his success, but he had gone out with his mother. He is a remarkable and masterly pianist. Well, our musical world has at last done a sensible thing; it has given me fresh strength. If it had not been for the pleasure I have derived from it I could not have written you so long a letter.

CXXXV.

JUNE 30, 1867.

MY DEAR HUMBERT,

A terrible blow has fallen upon me. My poor son, captain of a large ship, and only thirty-three years of age, has just died at Havannah.

CXXXVI.

MONDAY, JULY 15, 1867.

MY DEAR, INCOMPARABLE FRIEND,

I am writing a few lines to you since you so wish, but it is not right of me to sadden you. I suffer so frightfully from the increase of my neuralgia in the intestines that I do not know how I remain alive. I have scarcely enough intelligence left to attend to the affairs of my poor Louis, about which the agents of the Compagnie Transatlantique are consulting me. A friend of his has fortunately helped me in the matter. Thank you for your letter, which did me a world of good this morning. My pain absorbs every other feeling, but you will forgive me. I can feel clearly that I am stupid. I only think of going to sleep.

CXXXVII.

PARIS, SUNDAY, JULY 28, 1867.

MY DEAR HUMBERT,

As soon as ever I received your letter I got up and went to the celebrated counsel, Nogent Saint-Laurent, for whom the Emperor has as much affection as esteem, and upon whose friendship I can rely. Fortunately he had not left for Orange, as I feared. If anybody can bring your business to a successful issue, he can. I have no doubt about his goodwill. If he wants anybody to help him, I will send him M. Domergue, whom he knows as well as he knows me, and who, in his capacity as Secretary to the Minister of Interior, will leave no stone unturned to achieve success. Nogent will write to me to-morrow. Good-bye. I will keep you fully informed of what goes on.

CXXXVIII.

FRIDAY, AUGUST 1, 1867.

MY DEAR FERRAND,

I have received your letter, but it does not say a word about the one I wrote to you en-

closing a letter from Nogent. I am uneasy
about it. Have you not received it? It asked
for immediate information in regard to the
place where your youth intends to reside, so as
to spare him the police. Let me know at once
whether you have sent this information to
Nogent, whose address I sent you.

I am obliged to go to bed. I am to dine on
Monday with Noyent and Domergue.

CXXXIX.

SUNDAY, TWO O'CLOCK, AUGUST 4, 1867.

I cannot understand your silence. I
have written you two letters, on Tuesday and
Thursday, returning your letter to the Emperor,
sending you the one from Nogent, and asking
you precisely what he asked, the *name of the*
place where your *protégé* intends to reside.
Nogent says that this information is necessary
to obviate any *surveillance* on the part of the
police. As I did not receive any reply to this
triple letter I wrote you a second time, and you
have not even replied to that. There is not a
moment to be lost now. Send your information to M. Nogent Saint-Laurent, Deputy, No.
6, Rue de Vernueil. If you cannot write, Madame
Ferrand can.

I shall see Nogent and Domergue to-morrow.

I ought to start this evening for Néris, whither I am imperatively sent to take the waters, but I will wait for your reply until Wednesday.

Good-bye; I am extremely anxious, and I am in bed.

CXL.

October 8, 1867.

My Dear Humbert,

When I suffer excessively (and one always is suffering excessively), I have some wonderful distractions; you are like myself. You wrote to me on the 27th of September, but I only received your letter this morning, because you addressed it to Rue des Colonnes, Lyon. What the devil possessed you to do that? Fortunately, the post office administration is not utterly devoid of intelligence, and the letter eventually found me at the Rue de Calais, Paris. I was very uneasy in consequence of not hearing from you, and I was going to write to you to-day. You mis-read the letter from M. Domergue; he did not say *ce maudit garçon*, but *ce malheureux jeune homme*; that is a very different thing. Well, the matter is at an end now, and it is to be hoped that there will be no more question of saw, pipe, or blows.

I am on the point of making a master-stroke.

The Grand Duchess Hélène of Russia was recently in Paris, and she and her officers cajoled me to such an extent that I have finally decided upon acceding to her proposals. She has asked me to go to St. Petersburg next month to conduct six concerts at the Conservatoire there; one of them is to be composed entirely of my music. After having consulted several of my friends, I have accepted and signed an engagement. Her gracious Highness pays my travelling expenses there and back, lodges me in her own house, the Palais Michel, and gives me one of her carriages and fifteen thousand francs. I gain nothing in Paris. I have hard work to make both ends of my yearly expenses meet, and I have given way in order to secure momentary ease in spite of my continual sufferings. These musical occupations may, possibly, do me good instead of putting an end to me.

By way of compensation, I have obstinately declined the proposals of an American manager who offered me a hundred thousand francs to go to New York for six months. Upon that the brave fellow, in a fit of anger, has had a bust made of me, larger than life, which is to be placed in a hall he has just had built in America. Everything, you see, comes when one has con-.

trived to wait for it, and when one is almost good for nothing.

Good-bye, my dear excellent friend. I will write to you again before my departure. Remember me to Madame Ferrand.

CXLI.

OCTOBER 22, 1867.

MY DEAR HUMBERT,

I enclose the letter you want. I can only write a line. I took a dose of laudanum last night, and have not had time to go to sleep quietly. I have had to get up this morning to pay some unavoidable visits, and as soon as I have got over them I am going to bed again. Good-bye.

THE END.

INDEX TO SECOND VOLUME.

www.ingramcontent.com/pod-product-compliance
Lightning Source LLC
Chambersburg PA
CBHW060516030726

47498CB00004B/961